Die for Her

A Die for Me Novella

AMY PLUM

Interior Design by Woven Red Author Services, www.WovenRed.ca

Die for Her/Amy Plum—1st edition
ISBN ebook: 978-0-06-226770-2
ISBN print book: 978-2-9575891-0-4

Also by Amy Plum

Chapter One

The first time I see her, I peg her as a jump risk.

Vince and I are walking the quays, and there she is: long, dark hair whipping around her face as she stands on the edge of the cobblestone walkway looking down at the water, a mere five feet above the waves. The Seine is swollen from winter rains, so though the jump would be harmless from that height, the barely choppy surface could hide dangerous currents.

We head toward her, my hand already extended to touch her arm. To pass my calm to her, one of our only real "superpowers" as a revenant (or, as Ambrose likes to call us, "undead guardian angels with a bad case of OCD"). But before we reach her she turns and walks away, heading for one of the quay's stone benches, where she curls her legs up to her chest and ropes her knees in with her arms. She remains that way, hugging herself, rocking back and forth, and staring blindly across the river with tears coursing down her cheeks, as we pass unnoticed.

"What do you think?" I ask Vincent, who pulls his scarf up over his nose and mouth, shielding himself from the frigid January wind.

"I don't think she's going to jump," he says. "But let's circle around under the bridge to make sure."

We stride side by side until we get to the Carrousel Bridge. Even the indigents who regularly sleep under its arches have cleared out. It is one of the coldest days on record . . . at least since I moved to Paris a century ago.

We good revenants, called *bardia*, are fated to watch over humans, saving them from premature death by suicide, murder, or accident. Our job is definitely easier in weather like this, with everyone staying indoors. But even members of the reanimated undead can feel the cold.

Most of our work for the last few days has been rounding up the few remaining street people and getting them to care centers before they suffer frostbite or even death from exposure. Judging by her clothes and hygiene, this girl is definitely not homeless. Instead she's pretty enough to add to my girls-to-ask-out list. However, hitting on someone who is crying isn't quite my style.

So if she's not homeless, why is she here, taking a solitary stroll next to the river in the freezing cold?

We confirm that there are no stragglers under the bridge, and then turn to head back to the bench. When we reach it, it is empty. A few yards away, I see the girl climbing the stairs to street level. Since there's no one else around, we follow her at a safe distance, ready to run if she heads for the bridge. "Ambrose, use your foresight—do you see her jumping?" I ask.

Naw. The word skips my ears and goes straight to my mind in Ambrose's deep baritone. *But she* is *about to sprint up the rue du Bac.*

"We should follow her," I say to Vincent. "She's acting bizarrely enough to merit a few more minutes of surveillance."

"Agreed. She could still throw herself in front of a car," he says, concerned. "Something's obviously wrong with her."

"I'm banking on it being the result of a bad breakup," I reply. "That's what happens when people get too serious. Feelings get hurt. Hearts get broken. Some people never learn. Don't get serious. It's my number one rule." I rub my hands together and blow on them, trying to force hot breath through my wool gloves. "My fingers are icicles. And the streets are empty. Let's head back to La Maison."

Wimp, taunts Ambrose.

"Hey, if you weren't currently disembodied, you'd be agreeing with me, ghost boy," I say, and hear him chuckle. Vincent isn't paying attention and picks up his pace. I glance ahead of us and see that the girl has started to run.

We follow her, leaving a good half block between us: There is no traffic for her to throw herself in front of, and we don't want to call unnecessary attention to ourselves. She jogs up the rue du Bac, crosses the boulevard Saint-Germain, and finally turns left at a square where old, stately apartment buildings are grouped around a small park.

She walks up to one, and while opening the door, turns and casts a quick look behind her. Vincent and I duck our heads down and walk straight up the rue du Bac without her seeing our faces.

But I saw hers. And her expression is one I recognize—I've seen it many times during my existence. Especially in the line of "work" I'm in. The girl is suffering from terrible grief.

Vincent and I lock eyes, and I tip my head left. Toward home. He understands and we walk to the end of the block, turning eastward toward La Maison. It's not like we can read each other's minds. But when you're best friends with someone for over half a century, you start to recognize their every gesture. We're like an old couple. Words are almost unnecessary.

We walk for a while in silence, keeping an eye out for anything amiss. Ambrose doesn't spot any activity at all in the neighborhood and is singing a Louis Armstrong song directly into my brain, probably to piss me off. "Who is the lucky lady tonight?" Vincent asks as he taps the code into our security panel. The gate swings slowly open.

"Quintana," I respond.

"From?"

"New York, upstate somewhere. Over here doing an art degree."

"Blond?" he asks.

"Negative," I respond. "Dark hair with blue tips. Alternative chic."

"Sounds like your type," he jokes. We both know I don't have a type. "Female" is my type.

Like I said. We're an old couple—we need few words. But we couldn't be more different. Vincent stopped dating decades ago, not that he had been much into it before. "What's the point?" he had said. This was around 1980, and that year's bouquet of Parisiennes was breathtaking.

"What's the *point*?" I exclaimed. "They're beautiful. And soft. And they smell good. What do you mean, 'what's the point'?"

"We can only go so far, and then we have to disappear from their lives. It's not worth it if we can't even get close," he sighed.

"Excuse me, but I make it a regular habit of 'getting close'!"

"I don't mean like that," he responded. "I'm talking *emotional* intimacy. And why risk exposure of our entire kindred for a girl you're only going to spend a few nights with?" His expression was flat. Uncaring. But I knew there was an ocean of pain bottled inside him.

"Man, no one will ever compare to Hélène. It's been seventy years since you saw her murdered by those Nazis and you're still hanging on. You've just got to accept that your first love is your greatest, and everything else is going to be second-best. But second-best is better than nothing at all."

My arguments fall on deaf ears with Vincent. If he won't amuse himself with humans, the only other choice is to go revenant. And we know pretty much all of the female members of our kindred in France. They're like sisters to us. Revenants do occasionally fall for one another. It happens. But it just hasn't happened to Vincent or me. And until the next global convocation, we probably won't meet any new *bardia* beauties.

Which is A-OK with me. Why settle for one girl if you can have a lot? It's a good motto, I find. Works for drinks, friends, and women. Not so much for enemies. But our situation in France is stable. Similar number of numa and *bardia*. The balance of good and evil has reached an equilibrium in the past few years.

Which means I've got time to play.

Chapter Two

"Sad Girl at two o'clock."

I look in the direction Ambrose nods, and see the girl sitting on the bench, hugging her knees and watching the water.

"How many times does that make this week?" I ask.

"Well, we saw her last Wednesday when you and Vin were acting like babies about the cold spell. Two nights later she was back. Nothing for a day, then three days in a row. This is the sixth time we've seen her in two weeks," Ambrose calculates.

"And we've never seen her in the 'hood before. At her age, she's either visiting relatives, or has moved here. She's definitely not a tourist . . . not with that catastrophic look on her face and the fact that she visits the same boring place every day instead of going to the Eiffel Tower," I say.

We fall silent as we reach her bench and pass without her noticing. The girl never sees us. She never sees anything. She's like a ghost flitting through the earth without leaving a trace.

"No one's here," Ambrose says as we duck under the bridge. It's less frigid than last week, but even so, the number of poor souls daring to sleep in the rough has dwindled. Ambrose cracks his knuckles and windmills his arms around before falling into his boxing routine . . . bouncing up and down from side to side and throwing punches at an invisible foe.

I start to speak, and then stop myself.

"What?" Ambrose asks, executing a powerful inside hook.

I sigh. "It's about Sad Girl. Doesn't it seem like Vincent . . ."

"Yep, Vin's stalking her," Ambrose finishes for me.

I didn't mean to be that direct. I just wondered if Ambrose noticed the change in Vincent too. But I know he's right. Our surveillance walks seem to lead past rue du Bac more and more often, and each time we spot Sad Girl, Vincent insists on waiting until we "see her safely home."

"We're not Boy Scouts," I reminded him the third time. "We're not here on earth to help little old ladies across the street. No one's threatening to harm her, and she's not going to commit suicide."

"I know," he replied. "But something's different about her. Something's wrong."

"Well, it's not anything you'll be able to fix."

Vincent nodded, accepting what I said, but not liking it. He stared up at the side of the building until a light went on in a third-floor window, and then visibly relaxed, knowing she was safely back in her room.

"Who else lives in the building?" I asked, testing him.

Without thinking twice, Vincent said, "First floor: family with two small children and a dog. Second floor: geriatric couple, three teacup terriers. Third floor: our mystery girl, another teenage girl a bit older than her, and two elderly people. Fourth floor: family with baby and basset hound. Fifth floor's empty. And the top floor has lights on during the daytime. Someone in the building probably works up there."

"You've been watching people come and go," I said.

He nodded, looking guilty.

"That's not our job."

He ran his hand through his hair, stopping halfway through to yank on it in frustration. "Don't tell anyone," he said.

"I won't. But, man, you gotta stop. You haven't even saved the girl and you're getting obsessed. Flashing amber light, dude."

He shrugged, looking miserable. "She's a mystery."

". . . that can be left unsolved," I added.

But the problem is solved for us, because a week later, she's gone. Disappears just like that, overnight. And part of Vincent goes with her. For the two days a month that he's volant, he keeps disappearing. I have an idea of where he is. Haunting the empty third floor of a certain apartment building. But he never says anything and I don't ask. He just keeps getting more and more distant, closing in on himself.

March and April are busy months. We intervene with several suicide attempts (and unfortunately fail to rescue one), stop a few hit-and-runs before they happen, and rescue several victims of our enemies. (Not all revenants are good like we *bardia*—our evil twins are called "numa.") Through all of this Vincent has this kind of vacant air about him, and you know he is thinking about Sad Girl.

So I know something has happened when, in early June, Vincent returns from walking with Charlotte with his face lit up like the Eiffel Tower. "What's up?" I whisper to Charlotte as Vincent flits around the kitchen like his Chuck Taylors sprouted wings.

"A girl. Human," she says.

"Long, dark hair, pale skin, blue-green eyes?" I ask.

"That's the one," Charlotte confirms, stealing a glance at Vincent, who happily spoons a mountain of sugar into his coffee.

The next day I'm patrolling with Vincent when we spot her, and end up following her from her building to a cinema on the rue Champollion that's screening *Les 400 Coups*. She's changed since the last time I saw her. Her skin is lightly tanned and she no longer looks skeletal. She has been eating, obviously, and it looks good on her. She's still sad, but definitely looks stronger.

"Okay, man, she's safely in the theater. Can we go now?"

"Have you ever seen *Les 400 Coups*?" Vincent asks, his face total innocence.

"About fifty times. If you recall, we went to the premiere together in 1959. And no, we are not going to stalk her into the cinema just to watch the back of her head for an hour and a half."

An hour and a half later, we step out of the cinema, blinking in the sunlight as the girl walks ahead of us, making her way back home.

"You know what?" I say, not even attempting to mask my sarcasm. "That movie hasn't changed a bit in the last twenty years."

Vincent thrusts his hands in his pockets and does his hunched-over walk as we follow Sad Girl down the boulevard Saint-Michel. I grab his arm and yank him to a stop. "Vince. Dude. No more. This is getting unhealthy. I'm not going to say anything to the others about it, but man . . . you need to get a hold of yourself. Or I'll talk to Jean-Baptiste."

He fixes me with this soulful look like he's dying inside. "Jules. I can't help it."

I exhale. "It's okay, Vince. But we're not following her home. She's fine. Let's go check out the park." And he follows me up the boulevard toward Luxembourg Gardens looking like a boy who has been punished but is trying to be brave about it.

For the next couple of weeks he stops following her, at least when I'm around. I don't want to ask Charles or Charlotte or even Ambrose where he goes when they are with him. I don't want to call attention to it. Jean-Baptiste would be breathing down his neck if he found out, and we all know how unpleasant that can be.

And then it happens. We're at the Café Sainte-Lucie with Ambrose, sitting at our regular table, when Vincent's lips curve into a slow smile. I turn to see what he's staring at, and there she is, Sad Girl, sitting at a corner table, reading. She has this rapturous expression as she reads, like there is nothing she loves better than sitting outside, turning pages. Her berry-red lips are quirked up into an unself-conscious smile.

"Great," I moan, turning back around. Ambrose leans over to see who we're looking at and exclaims, "Hey, isn't that . . ."

"It's the girl," Vincent says. "But she's not as sad as before."

"Well, well, well," Ambrose says, folding his arms across his broad chest. "Why don't you go over and talk to her?"

"And say what?" Vincent scoffs.

"She seems to like reading. Tell her you're in a book club and invite her to join."

"A book club with one member. Good one, Ambrose. She's really going to buy that," Vincent remarks dryly.

"Naw, Jules and I could come and pretend we read the books too," Ambrose says with only a soupçon of humor.

"I don't need to *pretend* I read books," I interject.

"Man, movies trump books any day," Ambrose counters, leaning back in his seat.

"We are not having this conversation again," I say, but glancing over at Vince, I see he's not listening. He's lost in the girl. And Ambrose has the gall to look amused by the situation.

Sad Girl starts hanging out there regularly, at the same table in the far corner of the café terrace. Which, of course, means that what used to be our few-times-a-week coffee break becomes an everyday ritual. Sometimes twice a day, from what I gather from Charlotte and Charles. But I have more important things to worry about than Vincent and his obsessions. Lucien, the numa leader, and his crew have been setting off mini catastrophes all over town.

Over the last few months, the numa have gotten more and more active, and JB and Vincent are wondering what the numa chief has up his sleeve.

We saved a potential suicide from him a couple of weeks ago. She was fourteen and pregnant, and Lucien had convinced her that life wasn't worth living. As usual, he and his crew tagged along to see the deed done. To revel in their repulsive glee at having tricked yet another human to her doom.

I was volant, walking with Charlotte and Charles, and foresaw what would happen. I flew to fetch Vincent and Ambrose as reinforcements just as Charlotte and Charles began fighting Lucien's henchmen. Vincent didn't get to the girl in time to touch her—to pass her his calm—but dove into the river right after she jumped and saved her. Charlotte and Charles killed two numa under the bridge, but Lucien and another got away while Ambrose was fending off some curious passersby.

After that incident, Lucien seems to lay low. A couple of weeks pass without our catching sight of him or his men. Although all I want to do is escape to my studio and paint, I find myself spending most of my free time babysitting Charles, who is once again in one of his existential crises: Why are we here? Why couldn't he have just died and stayed dead? Why is he forced to live out this existence that he never chose? Sad Girl is completely off my radar.

So I am unprepared when Vince and I pass the café one morning and see her sitting at her usual table. "I could use a little caffeine fix about now, how 'bout you?" Vincent says, eyes glued to her face.

It's useless to resist. I follow him onto the terrace, where he takes a table a few rows away from hers on an aisle she will have to pass when she leaves. I spend the next half hour trying to ignore the fact that Vincent is only half listening to the stories I'm telling. So I amp up the intrigue and give him a story I'm sure he's never heard.

It was about 1910 and Juan Gris and I were leaving the Bateau-Lavoir, that hideous wooden building where we all lived and worked. If possible, it felt even colder inside the building than out. We were so frozen that even with gloves on we couldn't manage to paint, so our plan was to go sit in a warm café until our fingers unstuck, and then get back to work. Between us, we had enough cash for two coffees, and I guess we were looking pretty rough—but who wasn't in those days?

Anyway, on our way back to the Bateau, Juan and I got nabbed by the police. Handcuffed and taken in. We knew we were already on the police lists for suspicion of being anarchists and rabble-rousers (which we were not). But this was no regular roundup of indigents. No—these cops confused Juan with one of the robbers of the rue Ordener bank. They were sure it was him, even though we swore up and down we were innocent artists.

"Prove it," one of the cops said. So I grabbed a pen and paper off the desk and drew a picture of one of the Chat Noir cancan girls. But in my sketch, she had forgotten her costume, all except for the feathered headpiece. With a whoop of raucous laughter and slaps on the back, they let us go.

I'm finishing my story when I realize that Vincent's not even listening. He leaps to his feet and runs over to the girl's table. I turn to see Sad Girl standing behind two women who are gathering up a gazillion shopping bags, waiting to get by them to leave. But she forgot her purse—it's draped over the back of her chair—and that's what Vincent went to get. He returns with it, and has just sat back down when she gets tired of waiting to leave in that direction, turns, and heads straight toward us, toward the other exit.

"Aren't you forgetting something?" he asks as she passes mere inches away. She turns and looks at him inquisitively. "Your bag," he says, and holds it up on two fingers. She thanks him and reaches for it, but he yanks it back. And then they do this kind of strange dance where she's trying to grab the bag and he's pulling it away, insisting she tell him her name before he'll give her the bag. A classic pickup line that he has unabashedly stolen directly from yours truly.

Of course, unlike me, he fouls the whole thing up. In one catastrophic movement, she grabs, he gives in, and the contents of her bag spill all over the terrace. Her hairbrush lands on my foot, while Vincent picks up her driver's license and studies it like it's the Rosetta stone.

Retrieving her book from under one of the neighboring tables, he holds it up. "*To Kill a Mockingbird en anglais*," he says, and then launches into his near-perfect English trying to start up a conversation. "Great book—have you ever seen the film . . . Kate?"

Her expression morphs from pissed off to astonished. "How did you know my name?" she asks. Vincent holds up her driver's license, and she turns beet red. She won't even look at him and he's apologizing up and down, and I finally butt in to point out the obvious. "Help the girl up, Vincent, and stop showing off."

Vincent extends a hand toward her but she ignores it, struggles to her feet, brushes herself off, and grabs the hairbrush I'm holding out to her. Vincent hands her her book, and with a look that manages to combine humiliation with deep hatred, she stomps out of the place.

"Now that, my friend, was smooth," I say as Vince and I watch her walk out to the street and then glance back at us. Her face is now puce, but Vincent doesn't notice. He floats back down into his chair.

"Hey, spaceman, time to come back to Earth," I say, waving my hand in front of his face.

He pops out of his trance and looks me in the eyes. "Kate Mercier. American, Brooklyn address, birth date December ninth, 1991," he says in this awed voice, like he's just discovered the formula for turning mud into gold.

I shake my head in dismay. "Man, you've got it bad. But you know you can't *do* anything about it." I tap his shoulder. "Amélie and I are going out tonight. Come with us. I'll have her bring a friend. It's just what you need to get your mind off what's-her-name."

He shakes his head. "No, thanks. And her name is Kate."

Chapter Three

I'm heading up the stairs to my bedroom after a full hour of working out in the armory. Gaspard walks out of the sitting room and, seeing me, stops in place under the chandelier. "Must you insist on walking around the house naked, Jules? It makes me feel like I'm living in some kind of sordid fraternity house."

"I'm not naked," I say, pointing to the towel around my waist.

"A towel does not count as clothing," Gaspard chides.

"Whatever you say," I respond, and, yanking off the towel, drape it over my shoulders like a scarf.

Gaspard shakes his head mournfully and wanders off toward the kitchen, mumbling, "I am living with cretins."

Just then, Charles and Charlotte come bustling breathlessly through the front door like an angry mob's chasing them with pitchforks. Charlotte takes one look at me and starts laughing. I return the towel to my waist and ask, "What's going on?"

"Remember that girl who Vincent was following?" Charlotte blurts out.

"The one he talked to at the café last week? What was her name . . . Kate?" I ask.

"Yes, well, now he's gone and saved her."

"Where is he?" I ask, feeling a tingle of panic.

"He's volant, so he's probably following her home. A big stone fell off the side of the building above Café Sainte-Lucie and nearly crushed her. Vincent foresaw it and told me. I gestured for her to come over to our table, and she got out of the way just in time. The stone crushed the chair she had been sitting in. She would have been killed on impact."

"So it was actually you who did the saving," Charles interrupts. "Maybe Vincent won't get the energy transfer."

"I definitely got some—I felt it. Look, I filed these down to the nub this morning." Charlotte holds her hands out, displaying nails that have already grown past her fingertips. "But I didn't get the full surge—just a bit. Some of her energy definitely went to him."

"Crap," I say. "Whatever mystical forces created revenants, they sure complicated things by making us obsess over the people we save. That's all Vincent needs. Even more of an urge to follow her around."

Just then I feel a presence enter the room. Only one of us is volant this week, so I know exactly who it is. "Vince, man, you are so exceedingly stupid," I say.

What was I supposed to do . . . let her die? he responds.

"Of course not," I concede. "But you know what this means. You're playing with fire, man. And I don't want to be around when you come home with third-degree burns."

I know what I'm doing, he insists.

"Like hell you do," I say. I want to shake him and remind him of how much Charles suffered the time he fell in love with a human. But Charles is standing right there probably thinking the same thing, so I just grab my coat and leave to go to the one place where I am completely in control: I go to my studio and lose myself in my painting.

Chapter Four

Ah, the Marais. My favorite neighborhood in Paris. The vestiges of history within its two arrondissements span everything from the remains of a Roman wall to ultramodern art galleries. Whenever someone proposes walking the Marais, they know I'm in.

So when a volant Ambrose mentions patrolling from the river to rue Saint-Denis, I jump at the chance. It's easy to talk Vincent into coming along because he's still mooning about meeting the American girl two days ago. I know, because every time he thinks about her he gets this stupid grin on his face, and he's got it right now.

We start off at my gallery, where I show Vince and Ambrose some new figure drawings I'm working on, then zigzag down rue des Rosiers through the Jewish district, up rue Vieille du Temple past all of the trendy stores, restaurants, and bars, onto the rue des Francs-Bourgeois with its beautiful sixteenth-century mansions, punctuated by rows of fashion and cosmetic shops.

We head north toward some shadier neighborhoods, specifically the rue Saint-Denis, where our enemies are involved in the thriving prostitution and strip-show businesses. And just as we're

passing the Picasso Museum, Vincent says, "Sorry, not inter-
ested."

"What's Ambrose want?" I ask.

*I was just suggesting to Vin that we pop into the museum for a
little lesson in Cubism,* he says.

Normally I would pass. I've seen every painting in there a million times. I saw several of them before their paint was even dry,
since Pablo's studio was down the hall from mine at the Bateau-
Lavoir. But I have been thinking about the linear quality of one
of his early self-portraits lately—which has suspicious similarities
to one of my own works from that year. And truth be told, I
wouldn't mind inspecting it up close.

Within minutes we are inside the museum, standing in front
of one of Pablo's Analytical Cubist café-table-with-newspaper-
and-bottle still lifes.

"It just looks like one big mess to me," says Ambrose.

"No, see, he takes each individual item—the newspaper, the
bottle, the glass"—I point each one out—"flattens them, and
then rearranges those two-dimensional forms on the canvas. It's
genius, really, but the point is it wasn't his idea. It was Braque's.
And the two of them got into this *how-Cubist-can-we-get?* compe-
tition until you've got canvases full of barely recognizable splin-
ters of objects. But did Pablo give Georges credit for coming up
with the idea in the first place? Of course not. Because he was a
narcissistic megalomaniac."

"Don't look," says Vincent.

"What do you mean, don't look? The more you look the more
you'll see how I'm totally right and . . ."

"No, don't look behind us," he says.

So of course I do. And there she is: Not-Quite-As-Sad Girl,
sitting there spaced out in front of one of Pablo's abstracts. I can't
believe it.

No, actually, I can. "What an incredible coincidence, Ambrose," I murmur, "that at the same moment you propose a lesson in Cubism, Vincent's obsession is sitting right here in the Picasso Museum. Nice one."

I hear Ambrose chuckle, and know he set the whole thing up. "This is not being *helpful*, Ambrose," I growl. "It's being *hurtful*."

Vincent doesn't seem to think so, he replies.

I turn to Vincent. "Don't go talk to her. I'm warning you. This is the last thing you need. You're too into her to make it a one-night stand, and having a mortal girlfriend is the *worst* thing that you could do. Just pretend you didn't see her, and let's walk. Look, she's looking down. She won't even see you."

Vincent just stands there like he's hypnotized or something.

"I am leaving in five seconds, Vince, and you are coming with me. Four. Three. Two. You're on your own, dude." I book it out of there. I don't want to stay to watch this train wreck happen.

I feel Ambrose's presence nearby, keeping up with me. "Just a warning," I tell him. "I'll get you back for this next time you ask me to come with you volant to the racetrack. It'll be the biggest losing streak of your life, man."

Vincent could use a little distraction, Ambrose says. *He hasn't gone out with a girl for years.*

"I think you will agree that there's a difference between *a girl* and *that girl*. As in Vincent's so obsessed with her already that he's going to fall. Hard. And then we have Charles Mach Two on our hands. Resentful for what he is, and making all the rest of us suffer for it with his raging attitude."

But Geneviève . . . Ambrose begins.

"Geneviève was already married to a human when she died and animated. That's a totally different case. Speaking of, are you still pining away for her, waiting for Philippe to die?"

Hey, I like Philippe, Ambrose rebuts. *He's good to Geneviève.*

"But you still want him to die."

It's not that I want him to die this very instant. It's just that he's got to pass away sometime soon. The guy is ancient. I just need to be ready when it happens.

"That's twisted," I say. A security guard watches me cautiously as I "talk to myself" while exiting the museum. Probably thinks I'm some kind of nutcase, come to splash paint all over Pablo's canvases. Not that it wouldn't be an improvement for some of them.

Chapter Five

I scrape the oils onto my palette: a mix of Zinc Buff and Montserrat Orange for her slightly tanned skin, Vandyke Brown for her long, thick hair, Venetian Red for her succulent lips, and Perylene Black for eyes like oceans.

Valérie lies on my antique green couch, wearing nothing but what she was born in. I stand ten feet away, near the window of my studio, letting the natural light illuminate my canvas.

I'm painting Valérie as a reclining nude, Modigliani-style. I miss the guy, even though he was obnoxious. Always drunk or high and picking fights. Doing outrageous things so that no one would notice the fact that he was dying of tuberculosis and avoid him like . . . well, like the plague.

There was that time we were at a bar near the Bateau-Lavoire, and he did a striptease in front of a table of "ladies of a certain age." Ripped off every last stitch of his clothing. Almost gave the biddies a heart attack. "Serves them right for hanging out in Montmartre," he told the policeman who showed up. Those were wild days, and he was the wildest of us all. But give him a brush and he painted like no one has or ever will. Touched by angels.

Breathed on by God. And inspired by the devil.

I use one sweeping stroke to define the upper curve of Valérie's body, from shoulder to foot. She's reading a paperback, clearly bored. I only need her to look up at the end of the composition, when I paint in her face, so I allow her this off-time. "Okay, let's take a break," I say, and she stands, her soft, curvy body as exquisite as the Venus de Milo, as fresh as a ripe peach.

I will never tire of looking at women. Appreciating their beauty. Reveling in each girl's individual charm. There's nothing more beautiful on earth. And even more tantalizing are the ones you can't touch, like Valérie: I never mix business with pleasure. And not just because of security. (Lovers aren't allowed into our permanent residences.) No, it was a hard-earned lesson after a few catastrophic encounters. All you need is for one model to see another painted in a suggestive pose, and voilà—you've got a catfight in the middle of your painting exhibition.

Valérie scoops up a robe and drapes it lazily around her before picking her book back up and lying on her stomach to read. I walk back to the bathroom to wash out my brushes, and hear the front door open and close and Valérie talking to someone. It's Vincent. Good—I've been trying to reach him all afternoon.

I step out of the dark bathroom into the sun-drenched studio to see Sad Girl—Kate—standing in front of the window, backlit by the warm sun of the summer afternoon. She looks like a saint from a medieval painting: pure, beautiful, glorious, crowned with rays of golden light.

But she is not a saint. She's a hundred percent human, and totally falls into the "lover" category. She shouldn't be here with Vincent. I manage to tear my eyes from her to see Vincent standing by her side, looking like his head's about to explode.

"Kate, this is Jules. Jules, Kate," he spits out as fast as his mouth will move. "Listen, Jules, Kate and I were walking around the

Village Saint-Paul and I saw *someone* there," he says, raising his eyebrows. I can tell from his tone that *someone* is not just anyone and that a numa must be mere blocks away.

"Outside," I order, frowning at Kate as I usher Vincent out to the staircase and close the door behind us. Before I can say anything, Vincent launches into the story. Lucien and one of his guards were sitting at a café with some unlucky human—a businessman, from the looks of him. And from the pitiful look on his face, the numa had probably ruined him financially and were going to blackmail him or something.

"And you just left him there?" I ask.

"I had to," Vincent responds. "It's not like I can fight two numa alone and in public. I can't do anything without backup." He's upset. There was his archenemy working his evil ways with an unsuspecting human, and Vincent was powerless to intervene.

"I'm with you now," I reassure him, "and Ambrose can be our third."

Vince pulls out his phone and speed-dials Gaspard, telling him to send Ambrose to my studio. "He's on his way," he confirms.

"Good. Now you can tell me . . . why the hell did you bring her with you?" I cross my arms to control myself; I'm so tempted to throttle him.

"I'm not on duty twenty-four seven. She's with me because we're on a date."

"That is exactly why she should not be here."

"JB only said we couldn't bring people *home*," Vincent says. "I don't see why she can't come here."

"Dude. Anywhere we have a permanent address is off-limits for . . . 'dates.' Or whatever. You know the rules."

"Valérie's here," Vincent protests.

"I don't *date* Valérie, or else she wouldn't be here. In any case, your date is over!"

He scowls like he wants to punch me in the face. And then he sighs and his shoulders slump. He knows I'm right. He takes Kate down to the courtyard and says his good-byes. She looks disappointed, but that's not my problem. Once she leaves, Vincent runs back up the stairs.

"Ambrose is here. He saw Lucien and Nicolas," he says. "They're making their way in this direction. But more importantly, Ambrose foresaw the human who's with them throwing himself in front of a Métro train in about three minutes' time. We have to go now!"

"Session's over, Valérie," I say. I pick up my coat and throw her the keys. "Could you lock up behind you? Just drop the keys in my mailbox when you leave."

"But I've only been here a half hour," she says, sitting up. She looks uncertain.

"Don't worry. I'll pay you for the whole three hours," I say. She nods, satisfied, and begins getting dressed as I follow Vincent. We walk quickly toward the Saint-Paul Métro station.

You've got exactly a minute and a half, Ambrose says as we jog down the stairs.

"Who's up this time?" I ask Vincent.

"Well, it was Ambrose's turn to die, but he saved that kid two days ago," Vincent replies.

"What's it been for you—a year?" I ask.

Vincent nods.

"My last was March. So you can take it," I offer.

No one's going to take it if you don't get your butts down there stat, says Ambrose as we emerge out of the hallway into the platform area.

"There he is—the guy who was with Lucien," Vincent says, and points to a man in a suit who is blatantly crying.

That's our jumper, verifies Ambrose.

The man places his briefcase on the platform and lowers himself down onto the tracks. "Now!" I say, and Vincent gets ready to run. But before he can, we hear a girl screaming behind us. Someone else has noticed the man on the tracks. I'm stunned to see that it's Kate. She's pointing to the guy and freaking out. Vincent looks at me. I know what he's thinking. "Let's go," I say.

Vincent runs for Kate, and I jump down onto the tracks. The man is sobbing, holding his head in his hands as the rush of wind announcing an oncoming train blows me back a step. The train rounds a corner and bears down on him as I run between the tracks to get to him. He's half a platform away: I'm not sure I can reach him in time.

The train appears, and to me it is like a dragon, solid, shining, and enormous: the yellow headlights its eyes and the wailing horn its battle shriek. *It's like St. George versus the dragon,* I think, *but this time the dragon wins.*

The man lets out a terrified bleat, and with no time to spare, I push him to the other side of the tracks -to safety. And in my final second, I turn to see Vincent trying to shield Kate so she won't see me die. The train is upon me, sparks flying, brakes screeching as the driver tries to avoid the inevitable.

No time to dive out of its trajectory. *This is the way of my kind,* I think. Death is a welcome mistress, but damn, is she brutal.

I brace myself for the split second of wrenching pain that I will experience as the impact takes my life. Vincent's eyes meet mine. I touch my fingers to my forehead in salute to my kinsman, and then I die.

Chapter Six

When my mind awakes, the house is quiet. I sweep through the floors, see who's around, and stop when I see Vincent alone in his room. He's stretched out on the floor throwing chunks of bread into the fire and watching them spark. An untouched tray of food sits in front of him. He must have skipped dinner, if Jeanne brought him room service.

What's up? I ask, knowing the answer has something to do with *her*.

"Jules. You're back. That Métro crash looked pretty painful. I hope you get extra bonus points for it." His voice is mournful. I know he's glad to "see" me, but something's definitely wrong.

I stay silent and finally he says, "Kate says she never wants to see me again." He crushes a piece of bread into a tiny ball before jettisoning it into the flames. "She thought something was wrong with me since I didn't seem upset about you dying."

A completely normal reaction, seeing she is human *and we are* immortal, I reply.

"But Jules," he says, rolling over onto his back and staring at the ceiling. "She's different from anyone else I've ever met. I haven't felt this for a girl since Hél—"

Whoa, whoa, whoa, I say, cutting him off. *You have officially entered the danger zone. You should be thanking your lucky stars that Kate dumped you. What if she had fallen for you, and you had to reject her? That would be rough, man. Rule number one with the babes is don't ever hurt them. Make them think it's they who broke up with you. And in your case, that has actually happened. Saves you from having to be an asshole later on.*

"But what if there was a way," he begins, ripping crumbs off the mangled baguette in his hand.

There is no way, I say. *Okay, there are rare examples you hear about from time to time at a convocation. A handful of stories from way back when. But man, who would want that? They grow old while you stay young? It's not natural.*

"*We're* not natural," Vincent says in a dead voice.

I ignore him and continue. *Plus Jean-Baptiste has forbidden it for the French kindred. You're only his second: Until you take his place, he's the boss.*

Vincent doesn't say anything after that, but I know I haven't changed his mind. For the next couple of weeks he skulks around, a ball of nerves, watching Kate from afar. Never going close enough for her to catch sight of him, and being careful around the rest of us to look like he's not stalking her. But I can tell he's just dying to see her face. And when he catches sight of her at the café or walking home from the Métro station, he looks all tranquil. Like he's only okay if he knows she's safe. It's freaking me out. I have a feeling it's going to end badly, but there's nothing more I can say. And in any case, my mind is on other things.

Whenever I die, I'm moody for weeks afterward. Thoughtful. I think about my deaths, run Google searches on those of my rescues who are still alive, see how they're all are doing. But the most important rescue in any revenant's life is the very first. The one that turned us from human into *bardia*. My first save is long gone—he died over half a century ago. But there are vestiges of him in museums around the world, and it comforts me to see the masterpieces he created after I died. Half of Fernand Léger's oeuvre wouldn't exist if I hadn't handed him my gas mask and died in his place.

There is a particular painting of his, *The Card Game*, that I love to visit, mainly because I'm in it—I admit. But also because it resides just across town at the Musée d'Art Moderne. And since I'm going on a month since reanimation, I make my regular pilgrimage to see it.

The painting depicts a group of soldiers playing cards—soldiers Léger said were from his own battalion. I recognize my pipe, but he made my face look like a robot skeleton. He painted me as an image of death, soon after I died saving his life. The scene takes me back to those endless nights of card playing as we waited for the enemy to shell our trenches. Cards were the only thing that could take our minds off our feeble hold on mortality.

And now death is no longer a concern for me. It is something that I crave. That I welcome. That I need in order to remain immortal. Although Léger was depicting his soldiers as automatons—easily expendable, easily replaced—the metal armor he used to represent our skin seems like a posthumous way of protecting all of us. Of making us less destructible. I know the wars affected Léger deeply, as they did everyone in Europe. But he left visible records of his battle wounds.

That's enough. I have had my fill of *The Card Game*—at least for this life cycle. I turn to make my way out of the room, and freeze in place. My heart is pounding like a bass drum.

It's the situation that every revenant dreads, and the reason *bardia* who live in small towns have to move every time they die. It's not supposed to happen in a city of two and a quarter million people! We avoid getting to know the humans in our neighborhood. We avoid making friends with humans at all (okay—temporary girlfriends, but that's different because they're . . . temporary). Because if a human sees us die and then recognizes us after we reanimate, we are up shit creek.

But Vincent made a friend. A friend who saw me die. And she is sitting across the room, staring straight at me, her mouth hanging open in incredulity. She gets up from her bench and walks toward me. "Jules!" she says, and her voice is a squeak because she can't believe her eyes. I have one second of shock before I'm able to pull the mask down over my face.

"Hello," I say, and cock my head slightly to the side. "Do I know you?"

"Jules, it's me, Kate. I visited your studio with Vincent, remember? And I saw you at the Métro station that day of the crash."

I give her the kind of smile you give someone you feel sorry for. "I'm afraid that you have confused me with someone else. My name is Thomas, and I don't know anyone named Vincent."

Kate takes a step toward me, and anger flashes in her eyes. "Jules, I know it's you. You were in that horrible accident when . . . just over a month ago?"

I shrug and shake my head.

"Jules, you have to tell me what's going on," she insists.

People are starting to look at us, and I need to diffuse the situation before Kate goes into a full-out hissy fit in the middle of a public place. But what can I do? I can't tell her the truth. And she's not going swallow my obvious charade. I take her gently by the elbow and lead her back toward the bench. "Let me help you sit down. You must be overexcited. Or overwrought."

Kate jerks her arm away from me. "I know it's you. I'm not crazy. And I don't know what's going on. But I accused Vincent of being heartless for running away from your death. And now it turns out you're alive."

Kate's basically yelling now, and I feel beads of sweat forming on my forehead. Everyone in the room is watching us. A security guard walks briskly toward us from the front desk. "Is there a problem here?"

"No problem, sir. The lady seems to have mistaken me for someone else."

"I have not!" Kate hisses, and does this fist-clenching foot stomp like an angry schoolgirl. She huffs off, out the museum door, and I shrug at the guard, who has lost interest now that the storm has passed. As soon as he walks away, I'm off, down the stairs, booking it back out to the car I parked on the rue Rambuteau. I know where she's going: Vincent had the idiotic idea of taking her back to La Maison after I died, to "calm her down." If she takes the Métro, I'm going to have to make record time to beat her back to La Maison.

The worst that can happen is that JB will turn her away at the gate, I think, but I've got a really bad feeling about this whole thing. Vincent is volant. If she insists on seeing him, we won't be able to produce a walking, talking Vincent until tomorrow afternoon. And Kate looked damn well determined as she marched away from me. She's not the kind of girl who's going to easily give up.

Paris traffic is working against me on this all-crucial occasion, and by the time I run in through the front door, Jeanne is arguing with JB about a young visitor he said was waiting in the sitting room with a note for Vincent.

The sitting room is empty now, except for a handwritten letter signed by Kate. So I rush straight to Vincent's room, and there she is, standing next to his cold, dead body and freaking out like an actress in a black-and-white horror film.

I can feel a volant spirit in the room. "Look's like the game's up, Vince," I say.

Chapter Seven

Kate's initiation into La Maison happens the next morning when she sees that Vincent reanimated and we tell her what we are. She handles it better than I would have expected. Not that I expected her to go running, screaming out of the house. But discovering that there is a whole world of undead superheroes existing side by side with the regular human world would freak most people out. Kate takes it in stride. Only seventeen, and she accepts what we tell her with courage and grace. I am officially amazed.

However, Jean-Baptiste is furious that a human who wasn't preapproved by him entered our house and learned our secrets. And while he's chewing Vincent out, Kate actually comes to the kitchen and has breakfast with us—not only a crowd of people she's just met, but people she's just discovered are basically monsters. She stands there at the door looking uncertain until Ambrose bids her to "Enter, human," and laughing, she comes to sit next to me.

She meets Jeanne, and I can tell that knowing there is another human in the room comforts her. And by the time she digs into the bread and coffee Jeanne serves her, she's chatting with the group like she's known us all her life.

When Gaspard sticks his head in and tells Kate she's free to go, I leap at the opportunity to walk her out. After she says good-bye to Vincent, I put on my very best nineteenth-century manners, bow, and place her hand on my arm as I escort her to the front door. And when we get there, I do what I've been wanting to all morning: I apologize.

"I'm sorry I was rude before today, you know . . . in my studio and at the museum. I swear it was nothing personal. I was just trying to protect Vincent and you . . . and all of us. Now that it's too late for that, well, please accept my apology."

She watches me quizzically, as if she's trying to decide whether I'm serious or not. And then she picks up her bag and slings it over her shoulder. "I totally understand," she says. And she gives me a lips-closed smile with a teasing sparkle in her eye. "I'm a mere mortal. What else could you do?"

This girl is oozing with graceful charisma, like a teenage Audrey Hepburn, and I totally get what Vincent sees in her. Knowing she'll probably be around a lot, I really pour on the charm.

I press my hand to my chest. "Whew—she forgave me." And I step toward her so that only a few inches of space separate us. "You're sure you don't need me to walk you home?" I say, lifting an eyebrow and giving her my most flirtatious smile.

She refuses, but blushes deeply—hot pink spreading across her cheeks. As usual, I feel a wild rush of success. I love flirting more than food. Or even fighting. And evoking a blush is one of the most satisfying results I can hope for.

I like this girl, I find myself thinking. *I'm actually looking forward to her being around.*

⁓

The next week Vincent comes home two days in a row with this grin on his face that's got to mean he's been hanging with Kate.

"So you're going to keep her to yourself," I joke with him as we jog down the stairs to the armory. "Finally we're allowed to have a pretty girl in the house and you're hoarding her."

"No, I'm not," he insists. "Ambrose is going as Kate's sister's date with us this Saturday."

"Um, excuse me," I say, grabbing a pair of short swords off the wall. "Best friend, here? The guy who is always offering to set you up with hot babes, and you *leave me out*?"

"Jules. Saturday. You're volant," he reminds me as he chooses his own weapon: a Japanese katana.

"Oh, right," I admit. "But that still doesn't mean I can't tag along. You guys could use some ghostly backup if you're going to be out on the town with two very distracting ladies on your arms."

Vincent laughs and faces me in a two-handed assault pose. "I knew you'd want to come. I was just waiting for you to ask. You know . . . grovel a bit after treating Kate so rudely."

I lift my swords. "Dude, I'm done with the groveling, and fair Kate agreed to forgive me my misdeeds."

"Did she, now?" Vincent asks, looking amused. "I can only imagine the way that you apologized." And he launches toward me, swinging his sword downward to strike my crossed blades. I pull the short swords apart in an upward thrust, sending Vincent back a step.

"Hey, pouring on the charm is what I do best," I say between breaths, and ready my stance for his next lunge. "What can I do? The ladies can't resist me."

~

When we meet Kate and Georgia at the Métro station, I immediately see a kindred flirtatious spirit in the sister as she coos over Vincent and Ambrose in turn. The sisters couldn't be more different in looks, but there's still something there that says, *We share genes.* However, it's Kate who attracts my attention. She's glowing. Radiant. No trace of Sad Girl left.

Georgia answers her phone, and Vince and Ambrose start talking about whether or not they should go to the place Georgia suggested, which happens to be in a numa-frequented neighborhood.

Hey, Ambrose, I say, interrupting, *tell Kate 'Hi, beautiful' from her ghostly lothario.* He laughs and tells Kate what I said, winning me my second blush in one week.

"Hey, watch it," Vincent jokes.

Tell her it's a shame she had to fall for someone as boring as you. Being an older, more experienced man, I know how to treat a lady. Vincent roars with laughter. "Looks like someone's got a crush," he says, and then relays my message.

Kate gives this flattered smile as Vincent reminds me that even though I'm technically twenty-seven years older than he is, at the moment, we're both nineteen.

We take the Métro to Denfert, then walk a few minutes down a pedestrian street to Georgia's restaurant, only to find a large crowd outside waiting for tables. While Georgia goes in to cajole one of her friends into getting us in, I decide to take a quick spin around the neighborhood. And within seconds I feel that disturbing, about-to-be-sucked-into-a-black-hole feeling that I always get when numa are around. I move toward the source of the unease only to see the numa leader himself—Lucien—walking with two of his men just a few blocks away from where Vince and Co. are standing. I rush back to alert them to the situation.

I'll go back and watch which way they're heading, I offer. By the time I return, Ambrose is on the ground, and Kate crouches beside him trying to get him to respond.

I see a pair of numa with a drawn knife heading away from the scene, toward Lucien. A few minutes and they'll be back with reinforcements. I get closer to Ambrose and see he is dead. There's no way Vincent will be able to lift him to get him out of here, so I do the only thing I can think of: I possess him.

Talk about heavy. Ambrose weighs a ton. Luckily he has the muscles to go along with the bulk. But I feel like I'm wearing one of those fake sumo costumes—stuck inside a fat suit. Kate and Vincent help me get Ambrose's body into a taxi.

And that's when it hits me how special she is. She's brave enough to stay with Vincent, even knowing what he is. But accepting one of the more bizarre details of our existence with just a wrinkled nose and not a full-on freak-out—now, that's impressive. It's been a long time since there's been an addition to our clan, so new blood, even though it's human, is a breath of fresh air. I'm looking forward to getting to know this unique specimen of girlhood better. If she weren't Vincent's girlfriend . . . But I'm not going to go there.

But something happens to prevent us from spending time with her. Charles saves a kid who falls off a boat. Gets himself mangled in the propeller. And Kate decides that watching him come home in pieces is unbearable. It reminds her too much of her parents. She tells Vincent that if that is what being a *bardia* is all about, she can't stick around to witness his own violent deaths.

She breaks up with him. He, of course, is devastated. Stops eating. Starts acting like his old self pre-Kate: robotic, emotionless. He tries to build a wall around his heart, but the hollow look in his eyes speaks the truth. His heart isn't even there to protect. It's with Kate, and she's gone.

She leaves an empty hole behind her. There was this feeling of optimism and joy in the house when she was around that's now turned into a void. Like Vincent, I feel hollow. Sad. And as the days pass, I begin to realize I've grown to care for Kate. Not as my best friend's girlfriend, but as someone in and of herself. And I realize I miss her.

Chapter Eight

I don't know what's wrong with me. It's Vincent who's lost his girlfriend, not me. But I feel a sense of loss all the same. It's not like Kate has been around all that long, but the times that I did see her really left a mark on me.

Out of sight, out of mind, I tell myself. And then I do the thing that makes the most sense—I call a girl. Nothing like a beautiful woman to wrap your arms around to chase the blues away. But even an evening with lovely Portuguese Carli ends up with me walking home afterward and lying around staring at the ceiling, feeling strangely unsettled until morning.

Vincent is punishing himself. He barely eats. Whether in training or, on a couple of occasions, facing numa, he fights like a madman. He doesn't allow himself to look up whenever we pass her house. Once Charlotte, volant, told him that she saw Kate a few blocks away coming toward us, and he turned around and headed the opposite direction.

One night we're walking around Belleville, doing surveillance in Geneviève's neighborhood, and I ask him how he's doing. Thinking he might need to talk about it. He turns to me with empty eyes and says, "You were right before. It was stupid of me to even try to be with Kate. The only thing that makes me feel any better is knowing that she's better off without me. She'll meet some human guy and fall for him and lead a happy, normal life. It's what she deserves." The words pass through his lips, but it's like a specter speaking. Vincent is no longer there.

I thank the gods that I've never fallen for someone the way he has for Kate. But though I applaud my good sense in managing my love life, something in me feels almost jealous of the deepness of feeling Vincent has for her. Besides the fierce loyalty I feel for Vincent and my kindred, I've never felt that much emotion for anyone. And secretly, I'm glad Kate's no longer around because something in me fears that I, too, would have become more attached.

I don't know what to do for my friend, so I just make sure I'm as present as possible. Not like he notices that I, or anyone else, is around. But I want to be there in case he ever decides he needs me.

The only thing that breaks the fog of sadness hanging over La Maison is Charles's erratic behavior. He disappears for long periods of time, and even his twin doesn't know what he's up to.

So Charlotte and I trail him and discover that he's stalking a human. For hours every day, following around this woman who turns out to be the mother of the child who died in the boat accident. The one he couldn't save. He watches where she goes, and slips into her building to leave anonymous flowers and gifts in front of her door.

His sense of guilt outweighs his self-control, and though Charlotte, Ambrose, and I each speak to him individually—trying to talk some sense into him—he's sliding down a slippery slope and about to hurtle face-first into danger.

The last straw for Charlotte is when Charles attends the child's funeral. She tells JB. After JB puts him on probation, Charles flips out. He yells at everyone that he's had enough—he wants out. And then he takes off. We search for him the next few days, but we can't locate him, even with the help of the rest of Paris's kindred.

It's about then that Charlotte overhears Kate's sister and grandmother at a café and discovers that Kate's apparently taking the breakup as hard as Vincent is, and her family is worried.

She sits across from me on my green couch in my studio, sipping carefully at the steaming mug of tea I've made for her. "Georgia even mentioned returning to New York," she sums up.

Why does my heart skip a beat when she says that? *Kate a whole ocean away? That'll just about kill Vincent,* I think. And then I realize that it's not just concern for my friend that I'm feeling. I don't want Kate to go. I want her to come back to us, even if it means that she'll always be at a distance from me—*friends, no more than that,* I remind myself. *But I do care about her. I even . . .* I push the next thought aside and say, "We've got to tell Vincent."

"Well, that's what I initially thought. But what can he actually do about it?" she says, concern furrowing her forehead.

"He's got to do something," I reply. "The only reason he's not fighting to keep her is that he has this misguided view that she's better off without him. Which may, in fact, be true. But he has a right to know that she's suffering as much as he is."

We leave my studio and zigzag down a labyrinth of cobblestone streets, past medieval wooden beam-and-plaster buildings that are so old that they're leaning. Charlotte slips her arm through mine and we walk companionably toward the river.

"Where do you think he could be?" Charlotte asks me after moments of silence. I know automatically who she's referring to.

"I think Charles is here. In Paris. Hiding out. Needing some time to himself."

Charlotte nods. "I wish he had never met Madeleine," she

mutters. "But he hasn't fallen in love since her, and it's been sixty years. I know it's stupid to think there's only one right boy or girl out there for each of us, but doesn't it seem . . ." She trails off, leaving her question unasked.

"You still love Ambrose," I say, knowing the answer.

Charlotte bites her lip. Her emerald-green eyes match the topiary labyrinths in the Hôtel de Sens's garden. As we pass, Charlotte looks out over the medieval palace's manicured hedges, and sighs.

"Have you ever been in love, Jules? I mean, I know you haven't since I met you. But was there someone before?"

I shake my head. "No," I say. And as I say it, Kate's face comes to mind—her beautiful rose-petal pale skin and deep-as-lakes aquamarine eyes. I push the image from my mind and reach over to ruffle Charlotte's cropped blond hair, then put my arm around her shoulder for a side hug. "No, Char, I've never been in love."

~

Vincent opens his bedroom door, and Charlotte pauses before carefully wrapping her arms around his neck and giving him a supportive hug. "Vincent, you can't hole up in your room like this. You have to eat. You look awful."

She's right. Vincent's face is drawn. He looks haggard. In the last two weeks he has lost weight, and there are dark circles under his eyes.

"Vincent, we have something to tell you," Charlotte says, and recounts the conversation she overheard.

The change in Vincent is immediate. It's like touching a lit match to a pool of kerosene—life flares back up in him and he becomes a man with a mission. "She needs me," is all he says, and that's it. He goes to Gaspard and asks for help, urging him to dig up every possible recorded incident of human-*bardia* relationships from the older revenant's extensive archives. Vincent's determined to find a solution. A way to make things work. Since Kate can't stand to see him die, they decide to explore the most obvious solution: Vincent must find a way to resist dying.

"What can I do to help?" I ask Vincent.

"Help me make sure she's safe," he replies. I have a talk with Ambrose and Charlotte, and we agree that whoever is out walking will pass by her grandparents' building, or make sure they're near the rue du Bac Métro stop when she leaves and comes back from school. And every night around ten thirty, Vincent leaves whatever he's doing and goes to stand across the street, watching her window from ground level until she turns off her light and he knows she is—for one more night—safe and sound in bed.

It's not like she's in danger. Vincent just wants any news of her we can give. And the only news we can give him is that she's changed back into Sad Girl. I hate to see her like this, robotically going to school and back with an empty look. I want to see the spark return to her eyes. Watch the happy glow return to her cheeks.

It's obvious how much she misses Vincent. And I know she'll only be happy again if he finds some way to get them back together. I find myself wishing that I could work that magic for her. That I could bring the smile back to her face. But I slap at those thoughts as if they were mosquitoes. What am I doing, caring so much about my best friend's love? I deny my feelings for her because they shouldn't exist.

I begin spending more time alone, drawing and painting. Disconnecting my thoughts, and letting my paintbrush express what I'm feeling. One night I'm in my bedroom working on a sketch of a woman who looks remarkably like Kate when Vincent comes bustling through my door in a panic. I flip the paper over and lay my pencil on it.

"She just saw me with Geneviève and . . . Jules, you should have seen her face," he gasps.

"Who, Kate?" I ask.

"*Who else?* Yes, Kate!" He takes a breath and starts again. "I was having coffee at La Palette with Geneviève, asking her about what she and Philippe did to make their revenant-human marriage work. Talking about it made Gen upset, so I was comforting her. It was totally innocent—you know how I feel about . . ."

"You feel like her brother. Go on," I encourage him. He throws himself down on my couch and covers his eyes with his palms. "Kate saw us. And from the look on her face . . . Jules, she must think that Gen and I are together."

I pause. "Is that a bad thing?"

Vincent drops his hands. "Yes, that's a bad thing, Jules. A very bad thing. She's hurt. I hurt Kate."

"Okay." I shrug, not knowing what he wants from me.

"Jules, you have to talk to her for me. You have to let her know that I'm trying to find a solution. And that nothing's going on with Geneviève."

No, I think. *You can't ask me to do that.* The last two weeks have been hard enough, watching her from afar. The last thing I need is to come face-to-face with her. To remind me of how much I care for her. "And you can't do that yourself because . . ." I prod.

"I'm not sure she'll even talk to me now," he says. He presses his fingers to his temples. "You should have seen her face."

Vincent is a study in pain. I can't refuse my friend, however conflicted I feel. One look at the desolation on Vincent's face and I agree.

"I'll find her tomorrow," I promise.

Chapter Nine

The park in front of Kate's building is silent on weekend mornings. *Everyone must be sleeping in,* I think. For an hour it's only the pigeons, a pair of ravens, and me enjoying the spectrum of autumn colors, of the changing leaves in the early Saturday-morning chill. After a while the warm, yeasty smells coming from the bakery across the street draw me from my hideaway, and I take a break to buy a *pain au chocolat,* savoring the flaky pastry as the chocolate baked inside melts in my mouth.

I wait another hour before I see her come out the front door, and then follow her to—surprise, surprise—the Café Sainte-Lucie. The café owner greets her and gives her a table in the front window. To avoid all semblance of stalkerhood, I wander around the neighborhood for a half hour before returning to the café. I walk silently up to her table and slip into the seat facing her. She's so caught up in *The Catcher in the Rye* that she doesn't even notice. I wait until she turns a page and glances around the room, and when her gaze finally lands on me she jumps.

My heart turns a flip in my chest. Now that I'm looking into those incredible blue-green eyes, I find it difficult to resist touching her hand. I sort through my various masks, select a wry smile, and affix it to my face. "So, Miss America," I say, "you thought you could pull a disappearing act and just abandon all of us? No such luck."

I can tell from her expression that she is happy—relieved, even—to see me, and my pulse speeds up about ten notches. I run my hand through my hair and try to calm myself. I feel almost nervous. What the hell is wrong with me?

"What's the deal with you dead guys?" she teases. "Are you following me or what? Last night it was Charles, and now you!"

Wait, what? "You saw Charles?" I ask, astonished.

"Yeah, he was at a club I went to near Oberkampf," she says, her eyes narrowing as she sees my surprise.

"Which club?" I ask.

"Honestly, I don't even know what it was called. There wasn't a sign or anything. Georgia dragged me along with her and her friends."

I have a bad feeling at the pit of my stomach knowing that Charles is still in Paris, but avoiding his kindred. "Did he say anything to you?" I ask.

"No, I was just leaving when I saw him standing outside. Why?"

She looks puzzled. I decide to turn the conversation back to the reason I'm there. "So . . . when are you coming back?" I ask.

Her face falls. "I can't, Jules."

"You can't what?" I prod. I'm not letting her off the hook.

"I can't come back. I can't let myself be with Vincent."

"How about being with me, then?" The words are out of my mouth before I can stop them. *Where'd that thought come from?* I chastise myself, and cover up by winking suggestively, and she laughs. I decide to push it as far as I can. Take advantage of the hole I've dug myself into.

Taking her hand, I lace my fingers through hers. "Can't blame me for trying," I say, and watch her cheeks flare scarlet as my heartbeat accelerates. Her skin is soft. Warm. And I am touching her for the first time—our first connection—and it feels like the nerve endings in my fingertips are shooting off sparks.

"You're incorrigible," she chides, but she doesn't pull away.

"And you're blushing," I respond. I continue flirting for a few moments, enjoying her reactions before forcing myself to come around to the point I'm there to make. I tell her that Vincent is pining away for her.

She looks down briefly, breaking eye contact. And then looking back up at me with eyes glistening with repressed tears, she says, "I'm sorry. I wanted to give it a chance, but after seeing Charles carried home in a body bag . . ."

I remove my hand quickly, and stare back at her, emotionless. I am no longer flirty Jules; I am Vincent's ambassador. I must persuade her to give him another chance. A voice inside my head whispers, *Are you doing this for him? Or for you?*

"I can't let myself fall for Vincent if it means having a constant reminder of death," she continues. "I've had enough of that to deal with in the last year."

"I'm sorry about your parents." I turn my place mat over, fish a pencil out of my pocket, and begin to sketch her. That way I don't have to look at her. To be undone by those warm, trusting eyes.

But with a few lines, I've transferred her beauty into a two-dimensional version of my dream girl. Kate has all of the grace and dignity of Botticelli's *Venus*, and that is how I depict her. My fingers loosen on the pencil, letting the image flow from my mind to the paper, and I look up to check her real face against the one I've given her, and for the second that my eyes linger on her own, I feel a stab to my heart and know I am lost.

I'm falling for Kate. How could I? My best friend is in love with her. And she with him. *You must never let them know*—the words sizzle through my mind, and I feel like I am bleeding internally.

Kate drags me back to the here and now. "I saw Vincent yesterday sharing a very tender moment with a gorgeous blonde."

I ignore her words and continue drawing. I can't look her in the eyes right away. She will see it. She'll know how I feel. "Vince wanted me to check on you," I say finally. "He doesn't dare approach you himself. He says he doesn't want to cause you any more agony. After seeing you sprint out of La Palette yesterday, he was afraid that you might have drawn the wrong conclusion. Which you obviously did."

I dare to glance up and see a flash of anger in her eyes. "Jules, I saw what I saw. How much more obvious could it have been?"

Part of me wants to shrug it off. To let her believe that Vincent and Geneviève are a couple. She is at a weak point—wounded and confused. From decades of experience, I know that this is the perfect time to make a move—right after a girl's been hurt by someone else. I spend the next few months building their confidence back up, showing them a good time.

And then, before they can completely fall for me, I come up with something that will make them want to break up. I plant a seed of doubt, make them think that it's their idea that we stop seeing each other. I act sad, but let them go their own way, and we both end up with a smile on our face, and our hearts a little warmer than before.

Kate is right there, ready to be scooped up and loved. And I'm so tempted. She is beautiful: not just her face—her entire being is lovely. I see why Vincent is drawn to her. I find myself imagining that I'm holding her, and it makes me feel dirty. If I follow my desire, I will betray the person I am closest to in the world. My best friend. My brother. And although I melt a little more each time I glance up at her, I fix her gaze in mine and tell her what Vincent wants me to. "Geneviève is kindred. She's an old friend who's like a sister to us. Vincent's in love, but not with her."

Kate draws a sharp breath, and I look back down at my sketch, breaking her magnetic hold on me. "He's trying to figure things out," I continue. "To find a way around the situation. He asked me to tell you that."

I study the drawing I've made of Kate, and then tear the sketch off the place mat and hand it to her.

"I look beautiful," she says in astonishment.

"You *are* beautiful," I say, and leaning forward, allow myself to kiss her forehead. Her warm, baby-soft skin. *Get out of here now, before you do something foolish,* my conscience tells me, and I stand and book it out of the café. I breathe in the cold winter air, and my thoughts are immediately calmed.

Don't look back, I think, and walk faster. I don't know what's wrong with me. I cannot be falling for Kate, no matter how I felt in the café. No matter how I'm feeling right now. I can't let myself.

Vincent's waiting for me in the front hall when I get home. "What did she say?" he asks, just as Jean-Baptiste walks out of the sitting room.

"Same thing," I say. "She can't bear to see you." Vincent nods grimly, as if he knew that would be her answer. He glances over at JB, who has stopped next to us and is unabashedly listening in on our conversation. "But I gave her your message anyway," I say. I turn to JB. "I have important news—Kate saw Charles."

"What? Where?" asks Jean-Baptiste, suddenly on alert.

"She saw him last night at a club near Oberkampf. Said he was standing outside. She couldn't remember the name of the club. But at least we know he's still alive and still free to come back home . . . if he wants to."

"Did you ask who he was there with?" JB asks.

I shake my head.

"We need to get more information from her." He looks solemnly at Vincent. "You look horrible," he states.

Vincent shrugs, and turning, heads toward his room.

JB crosses his arms and watches Vincent leave. "I think it's time that I pay Kate's grandparents a visit."

Chapter Ten

"Why do these smell like an outhouse?" I ask, holding up an old, crinkled parchment covered with scrawling in Latin. Gaspard, Vincent, and I are in the library combing through old documents that smell like they were left out in the rain and then shut up in an airtight box.

"Because they were not properly cared for before they came into my possession," Gaspard replies curtly. "Just look for the words 'tenebris via.' You don't have to try to read the whole thing." He's more on edge than usual, probably because he's got two library neophytes handling his priceless documents.

Just then JB barges through the door, and Gaspard practically leaps out of his chair in surprise. JB calmly walks over and picks up the paper that Gaspard dropped, and hands it to him, then looks at Vincent with a concerned expression. "I had a conversation with your young lady friend and her grandmother, Vincent. And I have come to the decision that, as a family, they are trustworthy and can be taken into our confidence if necessary."

Vincent stands, walks over to the elder revenant, and leaning down, wraps his arms around him, giving him a hug that is heartfelt, but obviously something JB isn't used to. He pats Vincent uncomfortably on the back and says, "There, there. I did it for all of us, not just for you."

"I know," Vincent says, his voice choked with emotion. "But thank you. It means so much to me."

"Of course," JB says, extricating himself from Vincent's arms.

"How is she?" Vincent asks him.

"As feisty as ever," JB says, looking bemused. "She gave me a real telling off."

Although Gaspard looks shocked, I can't help a huge smile from spreading across my face. Of course she gave him a telling off. I can only imagine JB giving her attitude, and her giving it right back. *That's my Kate!* I think with pride, and then do a quick auto-correct. She's not mine. She loves Vincent. And remembering that makes me feel like someone dumped cold water over me. I have to stop thinking about her.

But that's kind of hard when Vincent enlists me to come along with him that night on his daily lights-out-in-Kate's-room routine. "You're my best friend," he pleads. "I need your support."

"Vincent, I support you. I just don't feel like going out and standing around in the pouring rain." But one look at his drawn face and the dark circles under his eyes, and I grab my coat. "Let's go."

It never seems to really pour when it rains in Paris. You usually get a light sprinkle with an occasional shower. But tonight it's coming down in buckets. We stand outside Kate's building, Vincent staring up at her window, taking the rain full in the face, and me fitting as much of myself as possible inside the doorway, but still getting soaked.

"Oh my God, Jules," Vincent calls. His voice is barely audible in the downpour. "She's at the window. She's looking at the sky — out at the storm." And then he's struck silent. He stares intently up for a full ten seconds, and then slowly lowers his face until our eyes meet. "Jules, she looked my way," he says.

"That's great. Can we go now?" I say, wrapping my arms around myself. Unless I'm swimming or in the shower, I hate getting wet.

"No, I mean she really saw me. And I think she's coming down!" he says.

"Which is my cue to leave. Good luck, *mon ami*," I say, dashing out into the rain and clapping my hand to his shoulder before turning to go. But something inside of me does this little leap, and instead of leaving, I walk to the corner and wait to see if she actually comes.

And then there she is, face radiant as she runs out the door, drops her umbrella, and throws herself into Vincent's arms. He picks her up off the ground and clasps her so tightly I'm surprised she can breathe.

Suddenly I'm imagining myself in Vincent's place, holding her warm body to me, nuzzling my face in her hair. And a jolt of emotion knocks me back a step. One look at their joy and my heart feels like it's being pulled apart. Why am I so conflicted? I love Vincent like a brother. Being without the girl he loves has made him physically ill. So why does their reunion hurt so much?

That night, Kate stays at La Maison. Spends the night in Vincent's room. Sleeps in his arms.

And something happens to me that has never happened before. I feel the acid burn of jealousy and it overwhelms me. I leave the house, jog the half-hour trek to my studio, and lose myself in my painting.

She wants to be with him, not with me. She thinks I'm a joke. A flirt. Of course—that's what I've led her to believe. But she doesn't see through it, like something in me hoped she would.

My feelings for her are laughable. Ineffectual. Never meant to be. So why am I cursed with them? Why can't I forget about her? I have sacrificed my very existence to the whims and desires of fate. I am fate's slave, and yet it is mocking me.

I look in despair at the mess I've made on the canvas, and sit on the ground, my head in my hands. I must get control of myself. If things continue as they have started, this girl is going to be a part of my life. A part of our clan's life. And I have to learn to deal with it without showing my feelings. I have to get over her. I take my phone out of my pocket and call the first number that comes up: Evelynn.

"Hello, *bella*. I know it's been a long time, but would you happen to have a pot of tea for a poor, lonely artist?"

I go to the only thing that I know will make me feel better. Another woman's embrace.

Chapter Eleven

"Charles was with Lucien!" Vincent says as he bursts into the kitchen, where JB and Gaspard are having a rare dinner with the rest of us instead of eating alone. Jeanne laid out the good china for the occasion, and left us with a feast of *cochon de lait*, an entire roasted suckling pig that would normally feed a dozen people, but with Ambrose eating for six, will only last the night.

Everyone stops eating and stares at Vincent. "What did you say?" JB asks in a strained voice. "I just came from dinner with Kate's family. And she saw Charles with Lucien the other night. They were talking outside of the nightclub."

Charlotte raises her hands to her mouth, and moans, "Oh no." I scoot over and put my arm around her. But I know what she's thinking: Charles has finally done it. He's asked the numa to destroy him. I'm overwhelmed both by sadness that Charles's depression has led him this far, and anger at the thought of a numa blade severing his neck.

"But there's not only that," Vincent says. "Kate's sister is apparently seeing Lucien. As in, romantically."

"What?" Ambrose roars, banging his knife handle on the

table.

"Of course, she doesn't know who he is. Or *what* he is," Vincent says. "And he has obviously discovered our link with Kate's family."

Charlotte starts crying, and I pull her in toward me so that she's sobbing into my chest. My eyes meet JB's.

"I'm ordering an immediate general alert," he says, wiping his mouth with a linen napkin and rising from his chair. "We'll have the entirety of our Paris kindred out on the street looking for him. I promise, Charlotte. We'll find your brother."

But we find no trace of Charles or the numa, and two days later Lucien calls with an ultimatum. He has killed Charles and left his body in the Catacombs. If we don't come get it that night, he will wait until Charles is volant and destroy his body, damning Charles to eternal disembodiment.

We know it's a trap. But we go anyway. And although we manage to kill a few numa and rescue Charles's body, Lucien uses the setup to act upon an even more diabolical scheme. He uses Kate's sister to get into La Maison, and drags the girls to where Vincent's body lies dormant and empty—his spirit is volant at the Catacombs with us.

What Lucien doesn't plan on is Kate. Kate, who overcomes her fear and horror to fight him. Kate, who lets Vincent possess her in order to combine his strength with hers, and kill the numa chief. By the time Ambrose and I get there, Lucien is headless and about to be charbroiled in Vincent's own fireplace.

Kate is adopted into the house. She has finally won not only JB's full approval, but his welcome, and what I both hope and dread most comes true. My fear that Kate will be harmed by the numa is replaced by the fear of how I will react seeing Kate practically every day.

Chapter Twelve

"She's a natural," Gaspard says as we watch Kate float through the double doors into the ballroom wearing a floor-length, pewter-colored gown that makes her look like a princess from JB's time. And man, does the eighteenth century suit her well.

"A natural what?" I ask him, unable to tear my eyes from her.

"Fighting," he replies. "She started training with me just weeks ago, and she's already got all of the basics down. I show her a move twice, and she has it mastered. The rhythm of the fight is in her blood."

"Doesn't surprise me one bit," I say, and set out across the ballroom toward her, drawn to her like a bee to a flower in full bloom. Ambrose is playing Louis Armstrong, and couples flood to the middle of the room to take advantage of the danceable beat.

Kate is so lost in the scene, she doesn't even see me approach. I've attended Jean-Baptiste's balls for years, and I still find them breathtaking. This year he's done the room up in silver and white, and the entire space is illuminated by candles—candelabras gleaming on the side tables and the chandelier prisms glowing like diamonds.

I stand just behind her without her noticing, and our proximity makes my pulse work overtime. "How's your dance card look?" I murmur from just behind her.

She jumps, and seeing me, breaks into a wide grin. "Double-check your century, Jules. No dance cards."

I sweep her out onto the floor and, folding her in my arms under the glow of the chandeliers, I allow myself complete freedom. I hold nothing back, knowing that she won't take me seriously. "Kate, my dear, the candlelight does suit you so." She blushes and I savor my reward, brushing her cheek with my fingertip. Her skin is petal soft, and shock waves from the illicit touch course through my body. She glances up at me, questioning, but I give her an overblown wink and she just laughs.

I take her hand in mine and place my other hand on her back, and pull her to me until our bodies touch. I feel more alive than I ever have—like myself times ten. With Kate in my arms I feel like a better person. Capable of anything.

She is close enough that I feel her breath on my neck, and closing my eyes, I let my lips brush the crown of her head. Her hair smells like coconut, and suddenly that's my favorite scent. I squeeze her and she laughs and looks up at me. "Jules, you incorrigible rake," she scolds, and then gives me a smile that makes me feel we're in zero gravity. Floating inches above the floor. Weightless and timeless, and I wish this song would last forever.

I know how ineffectual my actions are, but I do them on purpose—to punish myself. I deserve the pain that closeness to her brings. I want to hold her like this every day. I want to be the focus of her radiant smile. I let myself pretend for the duration of the song, and when it is over I touch her face again and imagine that we are together.

My ploy—speaking only the truth—works so well that even after pressing her to me, holding her close, whispering flattery in her ear, Vincent only smiles at me and Geneviève makes an off-the-cuff remark to Kate that I'm harmless.

It's with a feeling of despair that I return her to his arms. I want him to be angry. I want him to challenge me. Because then the truth will be out and I won't have to hide my feelings. But he trusts me too much to suspect me. And I love him too much to hurt him.

~

Jean-Baptiste calls a house meeting in the library a few days later. Charles and Charlotte departed on New Year's Day for the south of France, and Violette and Arthur have already arrived to replace them. But they have gone to comfort Geneviève after the death of her husband, so we are only five: Gaspard sits fidgeting by JB's side, and Vincent, Ambrose, and I warm ourselves by the fire.

Jean-Baptiste takes a sip of wine, sets his glass on an end table, and addresses us. "As I have already mentioned, I am convinced that the numa have a new leader. Violette has sources among her contacts who will try to discover his identity. But in the meantime, I want to address a plan that Gaspard and Vincent have devised, which may allow Vincent to resist dying.

"As you all know, we have a cease-fire with the numa that prevents us from attacking each other unless provoked. However, Gaspard and Vincent's proposal would necessitate the *unprovoked* killing of numa. I am strongly considering calling off the cease-fire since Lucien already broke it by personally attacking us within our own walls."

"Yee-haw," whoops Ambrose, who jumps to his feet in anticipation. "Are you taking volunteers?"

"Calm, please, Ambrose," JB says. "I haven't yet taken a definitive decision. But I would ask Vincent to tell you what is involved."

Vincent pulls his chair in front of the fire and leans toward us, elbows on his knees, and hands clasped tightly together.

"The plan we've come up with could prove dangerous, and I want to ask you for your help," he says. "A few weeks ago, Gaspard and I found the information we were looking for, about something called 'the Dark Way.' It involves killing numa to absorb their power."

"That's nothing new," Ambrose says. "The power rush when you whack one of those bastards is half the fun of doing it."

"That is correct," interjects Gaspard, "but the Dark Way is a systemized killing of our enemies. It will potentially give Vincent the strength necessary to resist death so that he may fulfill a promise he made to Kate. It wasn't even a possibility before, what with the cease-fire."

I have a bad feeling about this. I understand that Vincent will go to any length to allay Kate's fears. *I would too if I were him,* I think, and feeling a pinprick of jealousy, push that thought aside. Vincent's asking for my help, but this seems dangerous on so many levels. "If you only have a few old examples, how do you know it's going to work?" I ask. "I mean, if it doesn't, it means we've infuriated the numa and risked precipitating a retaliatory attack."

"Violette has verified the authenticity of the Dark Way stories," Gaspard says. "She's convinced it can work. In addition, her sources warned her last night about possible increased numa activity in Paris starting today. Even though Vincent will be staging an offensive strike on our enemies, we will need to consider a defensive strategy to protect those coming to and going from La Maison—not only us, but Jeanne, Kate, and any delivery people."

"I'm ready to start," Vincent says, and his decisive tone leaves no question about his determination to make this Dark Way work. "Can I depend on the three of you to help me?"

"You know you can count me in if it has anything to do with

zombie slaying," Ambrose says, rubbing his hands together expectantly.

"Your wish is my command," I say.

"Great. Thanks. But please don't breathe a word of it to Kate. I want to make sure it works before I tell her what I'm doing."

"You mean she would freak out if she knew what you were doing," I state. Vincent runs his hand over his head worriedly, and nods.

"My lips are sealed," promises Ambrose.

Vincent thanks us and proceeds directly to strategy. "Okay, Violette's source is aware of a group of numa operating out of the Quartier de l'Horloge. Ambrose can come with me. We're going to scope it out and find out if we can provoke a confrontation without alerting humans.

"Gaspard, Kate is scheduled for fight training with you this morning. Can you proceed with that as if nothing has changed?" Gaspard nods. "And Jules, JB asked one of us to accompany Jeanne to and from her apartment today. Could you do the same for Kate?"

I nod. Vincent leans forward and clasps my arm. "I'm trusting you with her life, Jules," he says in a low voice. "You know how much she means to me."

Ditto, I think, but all I do is nod.

Chapter Thirteen

The next week is a study in massacre.

The first day out with Ambrose, Vincent kills two numa. The next night Vincent gets home around midnight from taking Kate to the opera, and changes from tuxedo into fighting gear within minutes. We're bending the rules a bit, the three of us walking without a volant spirit. But Vincent wants to keep the "experiment" as secretive as possible until he knows it's going to work, and will only involve members of La Maison.

We head straight for Pigalle, where a number of bars and strip clubs are owned by numa or their underlings. Usually—unless we're saving a human—we avoid numa hangouts. As Ambrose says, it's too tempting to put some steel through them, and up until now, ridding Paris of numa has not been our goal. Just as we don't expect to see numa ringing our doorbell at La Maison, they won't anticipate a tag team of *bardia* invading their territory. Which makes them easy targets.

Apparently the word hasn't gotten around numa circles about the two guys Vincent finished off yesterday, because we walk into Le Boudoir Nightclub around closing time and there's a numa standing right in the entranceway. He's huge enough to be a bouncer at one of Paris's trendiest clubs, but the bespoke suit gives him away as the club's owner. Our hands all touch the sword hilts under our coats—as if we need the introduction. He knows what we are. Gaping at the three of us like we're the risen ghosts of humans he's killed, he turns and runs to the back of the bar, locking himself in the office.

"Excuse us, ladies," Ambrose says to the two scantily clad dancers who sit on barstools, smoking. It smells like cigarettes and spiced rum, and the lights are so dim that it takes a few seconds for me to realize that the bar is empty.

"You're not likely to have much more business at this time on a Sunday night," I say and hand them each a hundred-euro bill. "Is that enough to make you get your coats and go home?" They grin widely, disappear into a back room, and in under a minute are scampering, fully clothed, out the front door. I lock it behind them.

"You wanna come out or should we come in?" Ambrose yells at the office door. He looks around at Vince and me and shrugs.

"Kick it in," says Vincent as we draw our swords. But before Ambrose can move, the numa comes out, swinging a battle-ax the size of a headstone.

Ambrose whistles as he jumps aside. "Now *that* is an ax!" he says, leaning back to avoid the swinging blade.

Vincent doesn't need my help, but I advance and let the giant take a swipe at me. His asset is his bulk, and the commensurate power he can put behind his swings. Luckily I'm a lot faster than he is, or I would have lost an arm.

I swing my sword, and he howls as my blade slices through his torso. He lifts his ax in both hands, ready to strike, when Vincent lunges forward and stabs him through the chest.

The numa looks surprised as the steel penetrates his rib cage, and when it meets his heart, he drops his weapon and falls to his knees. Grabbing the blade with both hands, he attempts to pull it out, but suddenly slumps sideways, lying prone in the growing pool of blood.

"Nice form, guys," calls Ambrose from where he's retrieving the battle-ax. He runs his finger along its edge, testing its sharpness. "Good thing he didn't get you first; this thing's a Grade A killing machine," he says. "And now it's mine, all mine," he coos, like it's a baby instead of a deadly weapon.

Vincent drops his sword, and his hands ball into fists as he absorbs the energy of the numa. He glances at me, and I can see the effect it's having on him—the dark gleam of the eyes and the evil-looking scowl as the power hits him and sinks into his being. After a second he looks like a normal *bardia* again, but one who's downed a few crates of Red Bull. "Ha!" he laughs, and grabs my arm a little too firmly. "This is going to work, Jules. I can just feel it."

"Ah, okay," I say, wondering if this Dark Way plan is really the best idea. It's not like Vincent's going to go all raving-numa on us, but the immediate effects of absorbing the dark power a few days in a row are a bit frightening, to say the least. "How many of these guys do you have to kill?" I ask, extricating myself from his grasp.

"Just have to keep it up for a few months, one every few days," he responds. "At least, that's what Violette and Gaspard calculated."

He claps his hands together expectantly, and then pulls out his phone. "Yeah, Gaspard. Ambulance needed at Le Boudoir, boulevard de Clichy. One-way trip to the crematorium." He hangs up and looks at Ambrose and me with a wild look in his eyes. Based on my numa-killing experience, it'll take an hour or so for the buzz to die. "Montmartre's just a few blocks away," he says. "Who feels like running some stairs?"

Chapter Fourteen

The next week when I awake from dormancy, Kate is the first thing on my mind. The regular bodyguard duty that Vincent has asked me to do while he numa-slays has made it impossible for me to achieve my goal of forgetting my feelings for her. I have the overwhelming urge to see her. To go to her house. To follow her as she goes about her daily activities.

I actually did it once. I sat in her room, watching her lie on her bed doing homework. Chewing on the end of the pencil as she considered what she read. Wrote notes in a messy script that was completely illegible, at least to me. At one point she lay on her back and watched the ceiling, and an expression of pure happiness crossed her features. Like she had a beautiful secret. And I knew that she was thinking of him. I felt dirty and sullied for spying on this intimate moment and left immediately. I never visited her volant after that.

Chapter Fifteen

"Vince, looks like that zombie hit you as hard as you hit him," I say, pointing to the fist-sized purple patch under his ribs. Vincent looks down, pressing on the bruise, and recoils in pain. "Holy crap, that hurts," he says, sucking air sharply between his teeth. "That's weird: I don't remember him touching me at all. I must have run into something when we came back up the stairs from the sewers."

After two weeks of numa slaying, Vincent is looking considerably worse for the wear. Violette confirms everything is on track, though. She says things have to get bad before they get better.

So I nod, and hold my tongue. I'm encouraged when Vincent reanimates looking like his old self. Although I have a bad feeling about this whole Dark Way thing, who am I to go up against Gaspard and Violette's brainiac dream team?

But I'm beginning to lose my willingness to help him reach his goal. The more Kate's in our lives, the more I find myself falling for her. The more I see her, the more I want her around. It's a vicious cycle, and it's making me crazy. I've begun staying away from La Maison and spending more time in my studio, just to avoid our paths crossing any more than necessary.

I shower and slip into some old jeans and a T-shirt. "Where are you off to?" Vincent asks, rubbing a towel across his wet hair.

"Studio," I say.

"You've been spending a lot of time there," he comments, throwing his wet towel over a chair. "You planning an exhibition or something?"

"No," I say, and follow him upstairs to the back hallway. "Just a special project I'm working on."

"You'll have to tell me when it's ready for the viewing public," he says, and clapping me on the shoulder, disappears into his bedroom.

Throwing my coat on, I head out the door, through the gate, and toward the river. This is one project that will never be ready for the viewing public. Or for any of my kindred, for that matter.

Twenty minutes later, I walk into my studio and flip the light switch on. The room brightens as the track lighting warms up, illuminating dozens of female forms. Their poses are all different but the face is the same. Painted from memory in scene after scene is the fresh-faced beauty. Kate.

It's the bargain I've made with myself. If I can't caress her body with my hands, I paint it with my brushes. Use my fingers to trace her lines.

I shuck off my coat and go directly to the canvas on my easel. Squeeze out the paints onto my palette. And carefully . . . tenderly . . . taking my time with every brushstroke, I sketch the curve of her neck, apply the crimson of her lips, form her face into a two-dimensional tribute to her beauty. Mix my oils to the exact shade of her skin, and spread it on the canvas with my trowel.

She is my inspiration. My muse. My obsession.

Chapter Sixteen

A week later, Georgia ropes us all into going to her boyfriend's concert. Since Arthur and Violette are along for the ride, I consider myself off duty and bring a date. Giulianna. Italian. *Bellissima*. Feline eyes and feline attitude. She's a girl who's used to being spoiled. And she is there for one reason. To keep my mind off of Kate.

We start out at Le Meurice, where with the champagne and vintage wine, I drop enough euros to pay the rent for her studio apartment for a month. So when we wander into the bohemian chic of the concert location, her smile turns downward. "What is this dive?" she asks, peering around at the red walls and leopard-skin stage curtains.

"We're meeting friends here, staying for a concert, and then we'll be off," I assure her, and then choke on my drink as I see Kate cross the room toward us. She's wearing boots, skinny black jeans, and a wine-colored silk top. And she's stunning in a way that Giulianna will never be; her natural smile lights her face more effectively than the luxury-brand makeup and expensive facials my date splurges on with her father's money.

I introduce the two girls. Kate leans over and whispers, "She's gorgeous!" And I respond with the truth: "She has nothing on you, of course, Kates. It's just that you're so very . . . taken." She gives me that *what-a-flirt* look, and I shrug. I speak the truth and nothing but the truth. And yet . . .

The band is good, but I don't even notice. My eyes are trained on Kate all night. As she dances with her sister in front of the stage, I feel like I could do this—watch Kate move, spin, throw her hands up in the air, and bounce around—for the rest of eternity. When she stops to throw her arms around Vincent and kiss his lips, my stomach plunges. *She will never love you,* I berate myself, and turn toward the bar so I don't have to see.

Giulianna's ready to go the second the concert's over. We take our time, walking arm in arm through the lamplit streets until we reach her building on the rue Saint-Honoré. She invites me in, and I accept.

The air in her studio is heavy with perfume. Giulianna drapes her coat over a chair and turns to face me. I lift her chin with my fingertips and touch my lips to hers. She's soft and warm. I pull her closer, feeling my pulse accelerate as she presses her chest against mine. She runs one hand through my hair and traces circles behind my ear with her fingertips. Our kiss deepens.

I close my eyes and I'm kissing Kate. I don't even try to stop it anymore—this happens every time. With every girl.

In the beginning I fought it. It felt wrong. Now I just let it come, let Kate take the place of Evelynn, Olivia, Quintana, Guilianna. And although each of these girls has something special about her that draws me in initially—something that makes me laugh or smile or lust after—none of them even comes close to her. With Kate in my life, seeing her on an almost daily basis, no other woman will ever measure up.

My phone rings in my jacket pocket. I ignore it for a second, and then, pulling back from Guilianna's soft lips, I answer. Vincent's tone is urgent. "Jules, we were just attacked by three numa outside the club. Killed them all, but Arthur's injured, and I just stuck Kate and Georgia in a taxi. Can you meet them at their house? Make sure they get safely inside?"

With Kate's safety in question, it's not a choice. I move quickly toward the door. "I'm sorry, I have to go," I say.

"No, don't," she says; the disappointed pout on her lips almost makes me regret my hasty departure. I pull her with me to the doorway and let myself out, pausing on the doorstep.

"Sorry. Emergency," I say, and lean down to give her one last kiss. "I'll call you tomorrow, Kate."

She crosses her arms and shoots me a pissed-off frown. "It's Giulianna," she says, and slams the door in my face.

Chapter Seventeen

Vincent's "extracurricular activities" continue, with Arthur, Gaspard, Ambrose, and me taking turns as his numa-slaying wingmen. And finally, after reducing their numbers by more than a dozen, the numa react. But not in the way we expect.

One afternoon Geneviève calls, saying that while she was out, someone broke the lock, forced her door, and turned the place upside down. Gen can't find anything missing, but JB and Vincent are going to check it out.

The first thing Vincent worries about is Kate. "If this is the beginning of the numa's defensive strike, they could go after her. Since Lucien went out with Georgia, they're all aware Kate's my girlfriend."

"Why would they be targeting you?" I ask. "No one knows you're doing the killings. You never leave a survivor."

"I'm numa enemy number two, after JB, and *his* beloved is immortal. Trust me: Kate's an easy target. Could you please pick her up at school and stay with her until I'm back?"

I can't argue with him on that. And I don't really want to. He's asking, and I'm not going to say no to spending time with Kate.

An idea strikes me, and as I pull the BMW out of La Maison's drive, I make a pit stop first and pass by my studio to do a little rearranging.

It takes a bit of cajoling before Kate agrees to sit for a portrait, but in the end she says yes. We park the car and climb the stairs to my studio, where an hour earlier I stowed all of the Kate pictures in the ancient bathtub, pulling the shower curtain closed to hide all evidence. I have replaced the blank spots on the walls with other canvases, and smile to myself as I see the bliss on Kate's face as she walks into a room full of painted form and color.

I close the door behind her and turn on the spotlighting. "These landscapes are going to be in a group exhibition next month," I start saying, when a crash comes from the adjoining room. I grab a sword from the umbrella stand by the door and charge toward the noise.

"What are you doing here?" I yell to a sandy-haired numa who is crouching beside my desk. As he flings himself upon me, I plunge my steel into his torso. I've aimed too low for his heart, unfortunately. But before I have the chance to strike again, he makes a break for it and takes a running leap, shattering my window as he crashes through.

Kate runs to the jagged opening and looks down.

"Did he . . ." I begin, trying to catch my breath.

"He landed on his feet and ran off," she says. "He was holding his side, where you stabbed him, when he ran away."

"What was a numa doing in my studio?" I wonder aloud, and then see that my desk has been gone through, and books and papers are strewn across the floor. Kate bends down and picks up a set of lock-picking tools from among the glass shards. Whatever the numa were searching for at Genevieve's, they didn't find. And my studio was the next place they thought they'd look.

I call Vincent and tell him what happened. As I hand Kate the phone and hear his frantic voice, I suddenly realize: Just one strike by the numa and she could be dead. If he had had time to pull his own weapon, that might have been the end of Kate. I could have lost her. Permanently.

She hangs up the phone, and I'm across the room in a second, grabbing her by the shoulders. "Kate, you're fine? You didn't get cut anywhere?" I ask, and then I fold her in my arms, squeezing her to me in my relief.

We stand in the middle of the pile of shattered glass. Kate is in my arms, and her heartbeat patters rapidly against my chest. And things, for once, feel right. This is where I'm supposed to be. With this girl in my arms. I don't want to let go, but I loosen my grip and she pulls back from me. "Jules?" she says, a question in her voice. Has she read my thoughts?

I drop my arms, but don't move. We are inches apart. I breathe in her scent—she smells like almonds and lemongrass—and feel her warm breath on my lips as she looks up at me. And I realize that one second more and my secret will be exposed. I will kiss her.

I turn abruptly, stride out of my studio and down the stairs, and step into the cold February air to wait for Vincent to arrive.

Chapter Eighteen

The next day Vincent leaves for Berlin to track down Charles, and I am once again tapped to guard Kate. But instead of letting me drop her off at school, she talks me into taking her to Saint-Ouen, to this crazy relic shop that looks like it's been open since the saints themselves were walking the earth.

Kate insists on going in alone. I tell her she's got fifteen minutes, so after almost a half hour of no Kate, I'm alarmed enough to barge in, sword drawn. The only person I see is a scarecrow of a man, who cowers and pleads innocence.

Kate bursts through a back door, yelling for me to stop, and then proceeds to introduce me to a mother-and-son team of healers who claim to have links to revenants. As in, all revenants—we're talking both numa and bardia.

I'm so mad at Kate that I can barely speak. Not only has she put herself in harm's way by getting into contact with these dodgy people, but she made me break my pledge to Vincent to keep her out of danger. She could have been hurt—could *still* be hurt—because of this. Who knows what these healers' ties are to the numa?

After having a yelling match with her in the car, she still doesn't understand why I'm so upset. And I almost say it. I could blame it on heightened emotion, but the truth is I'm tired of hiding my feelings.

"Kate, I care about you. You don't even know how—"

There's a look in her eye that stops me. It's a scared look, like she's afraid I'm going to tip the scales and throw this whole carefully balanced equilibrium out of kilter. *She knows,* I think.

I put my hand on hers. The look disappears off her face, and suddenly she's back to good-buddy mode. And if she *does* know what I was going to say, she's stuffed the knowledge back down so far that everything's safe again.

I make her swear she won't put herself in danger again, and then I drive away, only a shell of a man. An empty husk.

Chapter Nineteen

The next week all hell breaks loose. I go dormant, only to awake volant to find La Maison in chaos.

Vincent got a tip in Berlin that someone among our ranks is working with the numa, and a surprise visit by some numa to Kate's grandfather's gallery confirms there is a leak. As soon as I'm volant, Jean-Baptiste and Vincent have me accompany them. We question Paris's *bardia* all night long, but by morning we've gotten no further in discovering the leak. JB finally calls the inquisition off and tells everyone to regroup at home.

On my way back to La Maison, I notice Kate and Georgia at the end of our street, hiding and watching our front gate. I slow down to investigate, only to see them take off on a scooter after Violette, who has called a taxi. That in itself doesn't seem strange—Vi can't drive—but then when I see Arthur tailing her on a motorcycle, with the human sisters following him, I know something's going on.

I stay alongside Kate and Georgia until they park at the base of Montmartre and follow Arthur up the stairs. I've lost track of Violette by now, but decide to alert Vincent to the fact that his girlfriend's skipping school and playing secret agent with her sister.

Thought you might want to know that you're girlfriend's gone AWOL and is following Arthur and Violette up to Montmartre, I say when I find him in the courtyard of La Maison.

Vincent claps a hand to his forehead and moans, "Do. Not. Tell. Me. That."

What's up? I ask.

"Kate's got it in her mind that Arthur's the information leak, and knowing her, she's set out to prove her theory. I can't believe this." He roars off angrily on one of the motorcycles.

As soon as he's gone, Ambrose pulls up in the 4x4. When I inform him of the situation he bursts out laughing. "Man, Vin must be angry! You think I ought to go lend a hand? Help him cart the truants back to school?"

Only if you want to get involved in a domestic dispute, I respond. *We'll probably be able to hear them yelling it out from here.*

I accompany him to the kitchen, where he begins digging into a monster-sized breakfast and updates me on the *bardia* he questioned in the Paris suburbs. He isn't even halfway done with his meal when his phone rings. "Katie-Lou? You still at Montmartre?" he says before she has time to speak. "Has Vin gotten there yet?"

I move to the space next to Ambrose's head so I can listen, and hear Kate speaking frantically. "Ambrose, Vincent's gone. Violette and a numa killed him and took his body. They've got him, Ambrose!"

For a second I don't understand what she's talking about. And then suddenly I do, and I feel sick with horror. Violette betrayed us. *She* is the leak. The one working with the numa. And I think of how much she knows and how much power she actually holds; I am awash with panic.

Ambrose orders Kate to get back to La Maison with Arthur and her sister. He hangs up and says, "Jules. You can get there fastest—you've gotta go. Violette's in a white delivery van with Vincent's body. Left the base of Sacré-Coeur two minutes ago. If you can find them, tail them until you see where they're heading. I'll mobilize everyone, and we'll be ready to go as soon as you return to us.

I fly faster than I ever have before, spurred on by my panic. I arrive at Montmartre in barely three minutes, but I'm already too late. The delivery van is nowhere to be seen. I frantically search the neighborhood for any sign of them, but find nothing. Not even a lead. And finally, I have to give up and head home to give them the news.

I am in a state of disbelief and shock. How could this have happened? Why would Violette have killed Vincent? And her acting with the help of numa? It's all too hard to believe.

At La Maison, JB splits the Paris kindred into search parties, dispatching us to comb the streets for signs of Violette—or any numa, for that case.

Gaspard and I head south, and return hours later with devastating news. A numa we found in Denfert confessed he had been told that Violette took Vincent's body out of the city, and was headed south. She could be anywhere by now.

After giving our report to JB, I go to find Kate. I must make sure she's with someone who can care for her. I have to encourage her. To tell her there's still hope, while knowing that that hope is very slight. I feel devastated. I can't imagine how she is handling it.

I find her in the courtyard, sitting on the angel fountain talking to Ambrose. She's been crying, but hasn't given up hope. I want to take her in my arms. To console her and to be consoled by her.

"What do you think she'll do?" she asks Ambrose.

"Katie-Lou, regarding Violette, I don't know what to think anymore."

"If she burns his body today . . ." Kate prods.

"He'll be gone," Ambrose responds truthfully.

The mournful look on her face touches me to the core. She loves Vincent body and soul. He is her true love. She will never feel for me what she does for him. But I will never stop loving her. And I have to learn to live with that.

Kiss Kates for me, I ask Ambrose. *Tell her to have courage; we'll find Vince.*

He puts his massive arm around her, pulls her toward him, and plants a firm kiss on her cheek. "That's from Jules. He says to tell you, 'Courage, Kates. We'll *find your man.*'"

I leave. I can't bear seeing the pain in her eyes and not being able to touch her. To console her. I join JB, Gaspard, and Arthur in the library, where they are strategizing—coming up with a plan to fit every eventuality.

We wait all evening, but there is no word. Violette hasn't attempted to contact us. Spirits are beginning to fall when, just after midnight, it happens.

I'm coming down the stairs with Gaspard and Arthur when Kate bursts through the front door. Her eyes are wild, and she's panting like she's been running miles.

She tells us that Vincent just came to her volant to say goodbye. He told her his body was in Violette's Loire Valley castle being prepared for the fire. Then he was cut off midsentence as his body was immolated.

Kate's face is a study of shock. Her true love's body has been destroyed, and we don't know what's happened to his spirit. And yet, she is still strong. Most would have crumbled in the face of such news, but she ran all the way back to us. To Vincent's kindred. I am in awe of her bravery.

As Gaspard leads Kate to the meeting room, I know what my old friend would want. The years of finishing each other's sentences—the decades of speechless communication—allow his voice to come through as loudly as if he were here speaking it into my ear.

Kate is my responsibility now. I must guard her with my life.

Acknowledgments

My gratitude to my editors, Christopher Hernandez and Tara Weikum, for prompting me to add more color to Jules's portrait. And many thanks to my readers, who, when given several choices for revenant points-of-view, chose Jules's story to be written. He gives each and every one of you slow, affectionate bises.

About Amy Plum

Amy Plum is the international bestselling author of young adult novels, including the DIE FOR ME, AFTER THE END, and DREAMFALL series. Her books have been translated into thirteen languages. Amy grew up in Birmingham, Alabama before venturing further afield to Chicago, Paris, London and New York. An art historian by training, she can be found on most days either daydreaming or writing (or both) in a Paris café.

Die Once More

This novella picks up where the international bestselling *Die for Me* trilogy ended and follows the eternally irresistible Jules Marchenoir as he leaves Paris behind for a fresh start in New York City.

Jules is a revenant—an undead being whose fate forces him to sacrifice himself over and over again to save human lives. He's spent the last century flirting his way through Paris and, most recently, falling in love with his best friend's girlfriend. Loyalty and heartbreak have led him to choose a new life in NYC.

Chapter One

A new city. A new land. A new life. Or so I had hoped.

I left my friends, my country, the home I've had for a hundred years to escape a girl who has seen only seventeen summers. I put an ocean's distance between us just to discover it wasn't far enough.

We traded places: She's now in Paris, and I'm in New York. And therein is the problem. This is Kate's town, and it's like she never left. She's still here. She is everywhere.

In a week of walking the city streets, I feel like I've seen her a hundred times. From the American accents of high school girls chatting loudly on the subway to the downtown teenagers wearing her uniform of T-shirt, slim jeans, and Converses. She is in all of them, peering out of their eyes, taunting me with a love I will never taste. Because her heart is with another—my best friend, Vincent. I love him like a brother, but right now couldn't be gladder about the four thousand miles of ocean between us.

I wrap my coat tighter around me and lean out over my rooftop vantage point. Below me, chunks of floating ice turn the East River into one of the frozen martinis that seem to be endlessly flowing at my New York kindred's parties. For a bitingly cold daybreak the first week of March, the Paris sky would be spread with a blanket of gray clouds. But here in Brooklyn, where the sun has just risen, the sky is a dazzling field of cornflowers. The diamonds it casts on the surface of the water blind me. Bring me to tears. Or at least, provide a good excuse for my stinging eyes.

I hear a whistle, and turn to see my kindred Faust waiting for me next to a door shaft sticking up like a lone tombstone in the middle of the football-field-size roof. I make my way toward him, passing the barbecue pits and the giant swimming pool: all covered and hibernating. Waiting for the ice to melt and the city to move the party back outside again. The endless party. Life's a party in New York.

What am I doing here? I ask myself for the hundredth time. *Surviving,* is the correct response. *The only way I know how.*

"Council's ready for you," Faust says, clapping me across the shoulder as he guides me down the stairs.

"So I don't get it," he says. "You and your kindred come to New York a week ago on a mission to re-embody your kindred Vincent. You succeed, he goes back with the others, but you decide to hang out here at Frank and Myra's house. Then Vincent calls you to Paris, and after barely twenty-four hours in France you're back in New York?"

"What can I say? They were up against Violette and her army," I say, avoiding his point.

Faust nods. "Yeah, I guess you can't turn down a request from your kindred to help out with Paris's final battle against the numa. Man, what I would have given to be there and watch the Champion kick numa ass."

"It was a spur-of-the-moment thing," I respond. "Only room for twelve on Gold's plane. I would have brought more of you if I had understood what was going down."

"Frank and Myra . . . they're still in Paris, right?" Faust asks, eyes sparkling with good-natured jealousy. "I can't understand why you came back last night and didn't stick around for the after-party," he says, and then, seeing my blank expression, shuts up.

After a few seconds, he murmurs, "Man, we could sure use your Champion here. We've got our own bad stuff going down. But I'm sure you've heard all about that."

I follow him down six long flights of stairs. This building is massive, taking up a whole city block. Faust explains the floor plan as we descend.

"So you've already seen the roof. Next floor down, the seventh floor, is exhibition space, concert hall, and—as you probably saw last night—party headquarters. It's the only floor allowed to humans. That's why it has a dedicated elevator and stairway that don't access the other levels."

Faust points to a wall where industrial-size elevator cars are caged in by retracting metal gates. "Those go down to the basement. Man, you have to see that. It's so huge, there are actually two antique railroad tracks down there—used to bring goods in and out. At the front of the building we have river access for boats, and a dozen ambulances. The armory's down there too. Basically everything that's high security, and the stuff we don't want people to see, is belowground."

We exit the stairwell on the ground floor and begin making our way down the cavernous stone-gray corridors toward the front of the building. As we walk, I try to get a reading on Faust. He's got this regimented air, but not as much as a soldier or policeman. And he struts straight-backed, but with his arms slightly spread, like his muscles are getting in the way. He's already built big but has doubled his size with some serious time in the gym. Like most guys I've seen here, he favors facial hair: long razor stubble for him. Taking a wild guess, I would peg him as a fireman. I wonder if that's what he was before he died.

"So I've given you the layout. Now let me explain what it's all about," Faust says, switching into tour guide mode. "The building's a New York landmark, built of reinforced concrete in 1913 for a food processing company and then abandoned in the fifties."

I nod, and he continues. "Gold scooped it up for a song and made it our secret headquarters. No one realized we were operating out of here until the nineties . . . at which point it was decided to make it an open secret."

We turn a corner, and I begin to hear voices echoing through the cavernous corridors. "To the community, we're a bunch of artists, musicians, and young independent businesspeople—creative types—who've been granted these luxury living and working spaces by an arts foundation. We 'give back to the community' by opening the place up for exhibitions, concerts, and the monthly intel-gathering 'block parties' like we had last night."

He smiles at the memory of the epic party on the top floor of the building that just ended a few hours ago. It was in full swing when I arrived from the airport. I passed through, grabbed a drink, and spent the rest of the evening alone on the roof, until, after dawn, I saw the fleet of revenant-driven taxis shuttle the last partygoers home.

No partying for me. Not last night. Not with the gore of battle still fresh in my mind. Not after witnessing the permanent death of Jean-Baptiste, our leader. And in the midst of it all, my lovely Kate, fierce and beautiful and no longer human. I needed time to process it. To remember. To heal.

"It's the best spy network ever," Faust explains, jerking me back into the here and now. "The locals offer us up valuable information on our enemies without even knowing what they're giving us. The council always meets immediately after to discuss what we learned. So—perfect timing for your official welcome." Faust and I turn a corner and are in an airy, sunlit space occupying the entire front section of the building, overlooking the waterfront. A kitchen that could easily provide for several restaurants is fitted along the wall at the back. And between it and the floor-to-ceiling windows is a café area with around fifty tables. These are artfully grouped around potted trees strung with Christmas lights.

"This is where I leave you," Faust says, gesturing toward a gathering of ten tables arranged in a large circle. Several dozen of my New York kindred are seated there, waiting for me in a solemn silence. I move to stand behind the one empty chair left at the "head" of the circle—the one with the prime view of the river.

A familiar figure, dressed all in white, stands at the far end of the table to greet me. "Bardia of the five boroughs of New York, I present to you Jules Marchenoir, longtime Paris kindred," says Theodore Gold. "Witness for yourselves: His aura confirms him as one of us. Having met him before, I personally vouch for his goodwill, and I know that he is highly esteemed by the kindred of his birthplace."

"And *I* personally vouch for this man's ability to seduce half the human population of London without even breaking a sweat," interrupts a muscle-bound guy who could be Ambrose's older brother, drawing laughs from around the table. He holds up a fist, which I bump with my own as I take my seat next to him. "Met you at the '97 London convocation. Coleman Bailey, Harlem Riots of '43," he says, repeating a tradition I'd noticed with American revenants: introducing themselves with a detail of their death.

Gold chuckles, taking his seat, and says, "Sorry for the formal tone, Jules. There's a formula for introducing out-of-town revenants to kindred. Besides having a high number of immigrants, Americans also tend to move around a lot."

I nod and accept a glass and pitcher of water from the man sitting on my left. "We're used to formalities in the Old World," I say, trying my best to sound light. This is the last place I want to be: in the hot seat, having to explain myself to a lot of strangers while my brain is melting and my heart is in tiny jagged pieces—in a language that is not my own. But it's a necessary evil. If I want to stay, they need to know why.

My face has given something away: I see compassion on my kindred's faces. One girl speaks up. "We were so sorry to hear about Jean-Baptiste," she says, and everyone else nods and adds their own words of condolence.

Gold speaks up. "We're going to make this brief, Jules. No formal inquisition necessary. In America we don't have leaders or 'heads' like you do in Europe. Everything is done democratically. I usually speak for the crowd, since I am the official American historian—somewhat like Gaspard is for you. But any New York revenant animated over twenty years can be on the council, and it holds all the power."

Gold pauses and looks around the group, waiting to see if anyone wants to jump in. When no one does, he says, "You have expressed a desire to join us here in New York. Could you give us an indication of how long you plan on staying?"

Here we go. "An indeterminate amount of time, if you are willing to host me," I respond.

I see curiosity burn behind the eyes of the bardia. A member of the council speaks up. "Can you tell us the purpose of your stay?"

"I need time away from Paris," I say.

"Wouldn't your kindred prefer you to stay closer . . . say,

elsewhere in France?" she presses.

"At the moment, I was hoping for a bit more ... distance." This is harder than I thought. If I could say it in French, I could add the innuendos needed to imply that it was a personal issue and they could mind their own damn business. But their expressions show openness and willingness to help me, so I swallow my bitterness. Note to self: They're not the ones I'm upset with.

"Your kindred called you back to France to fight with them barely two days ago," someone says, "and you complied. But you returned to New York last night—immediately after the battle. Can we conclude that this break from France is your decision, and not something wished for by your leaders?"

I take a moment to formulate my response. "My kindred would prefer that I stay. It is my decision to leave. But I am here with their blessing."

"We will not be perceived as taking your side in any type of personal dispute, then, if we welcome you among us?"

"Definitely not," I respond.

Everyone seems to relax. So this is what they were digging for.

Another man speaks up. "Thank you for the clarification. Jean-Baptiste named Vincent the head of France's revenants the same day you defected. We were worried about becoming involved in a power struggle."

I shake my head. "Vincent is the best man for that job. I support him fully." They are awaiting further explanation, but I'm not going to give them any. I'm not about to announce that I'm here because I'm heartbroken. That the woman I love is in love with my best friend. That it will kill me if I have to see them together any longer.

Around the table significant looks are being thrown among council members, and there is a general nodding of heads. A man with a mustache and a strong Southern accent speaks up. I have to listen closely to understand him. "Frederick Mackenzie, American Civil War. I'm acting administrator of the Warehouse. So far, you've been staying in the Greenpoint house. Gold says he put you there temporarily, since you knew Frank and Myra from a convocation. But we ask all newcomers to the New York clan— whether you're freshly animated or an old-timer from out of town—to live here in headquarters for the first six months. That way you can learn our ways without being an unwitting security risk just because you did things differently back home. After the six months, you are welcome to join a house in the borough of your choice, or, like many of our more sociable kindred, decide to stay here."

He pauses, and I nod to show I understand.

"Pre-council kindred often serve as welcome reps. Faustino, who you have already met, has been assigned to you. He'll be happy to show you around, explain the rules, and fix you up with your basic needs. Is there anything else we can do to make your transition to America easier?"

I'm not sure what to say. They're so . . . efficient.

A woman sitting next to Gold jumps in. "For those of you who don't already know of him, Jules Marchenoir is an accomplished artist. Perhaps those involved in the visual arts could provide him with necessary supplies, get him set up with a studio, and tell him when the life drawing group meets."

The woman is stunning—in an exotic kind of way: long black hair, copper-colored skin, almond eyes, and high cheekbones. I rack my brain but am sure I haven't seen her before. I would have remembered. So how does she know me?

"Thank you," I acknowledge gratefully.

She nods, but frowns, like the interaction is distasteful to her. Like I've offended her.

How bizarre. I must have met her before—it had to have been at a convocation. Did I try to pick her up or something? I doubt it—I restrict true flirting to human girls for just this reason. Why risk offending someone who could hold a grudge for eternity? Not to mention the danger of them falling in love. And who wants that?

Or at least that's how I used to think. Pre-Kate. She changed my game. Now I'd give up all the flirtations in the world just to be with her. Something pings sorely in my chest, and without thinking, I raise my hand to press it, drawing concerned looks. My kindred think I'm mourning. Let them. I am.

Gold breaks the silence. "Anyone else have a question?" He peers around the table. "No? Well, then I'll speak for all of us to say, 'Welcome, kindred.' We're glad you're here, Jules Marchenoir."

"Welcome!" several say together, like a cheer. People rise to go, several crowding around me to introduce themselves. Several ask about the French Champion—Kate. They want to know more details about how she emerged, and it is quickly obvious that their own numa problem is beginning to approach what we experienced in France.

My gaze drifts across the table to the girl who spoke earlier. A group of people stand around her, and the face that was stony with me is now radiant as she speaks with them.

A beautiful girl. Normally that would draw me like a moth to flame. Even with my no-kindred-lovers rule, a bit of playful banter and a shower of compliments (and the enjoyment of her inevitable response) would do my spirits a world of good. But not now. I don't even have it in me to say hello.

Her eyes lift and meet mine, and the coldness is like an ice ray. *What?* I ask her silently, shrugging my confusion.

She rolls her eyes—actually *rolls her eyes!*—and turns her

attention back to the person she's talking to.

Disconcerted, I look back to a man standing with his hand out and remember that I'm supposed to shake. No *bises*—cheek kisses—of course.

Faust appears and stands by my side as the room empties. "Need anything?" he whispers to me.

"Yes," I whisper back. "I would give my immortal soul to get out of here and walk.

Printed in Great Britain
by Amazon